Dear Reader,

Looking back over the years, I find it realise that thirty of them have gone by since I wrote my first book—*Sister Peters in Amsterdam*. It wasn't until I started writing about her that I found that once I had started writing, nothing was going to make me stop—and at that time I had no intention of sending it to a publisher. It was my daughter who urged me to try my luck.

I shall never forget the thrill of having my first book accepted. A thrill I still get each time a new story is accepted. Writing to me is such a pleasure, and seeing a story unfolding on my old typewriter is like watching a film and wondering how it will end. Happily of course.

To have so many of my books re-published is such a delightful thing to happen and I can only hope that those who read them will share my pleasure in seeing them on the bookshelves again...and enjoy reading them.

Betty Neels

Back by Popular Demand

A collector's edition of favourite titles from one of the world's best-loved romance authors. Mills & Boon® are proud to bring back these sought after titles and present them as one cherished collection.

BETTY NEELS: COLLECTOR'S EDITION

A GOOD WIFE

BY
BETTY NEELS

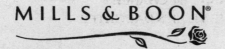

MILLS & BOON®

MILLS & BOON and MILLS & BOON with the Rose Device
are registered trademarks of the publisher.

First published in Great Britain 1999 by Mills & Boon Limited
This edition 2001
Harlequin Mills & Boon Limited,
Eton House, 18-24 Paradise Road, Richmond, Surrey TW9 1SR

© Betty Neels 1999

ISBN 0 263 82835 2

73-0901

Printed and bound in Spain
by Litografia Rosés S.A., Barcelona

CHAPTER ONE

SERENA LIGHTFOOT, awakened by the early sun of an April morning, rolled over onto her back and contemplated the ceiling; today was her twenty-sixth birthday. Not that it was going to be any different from any other day in the year; her father certainly wouldn't remember, Matthew, her younger brother, a curate living some way away and recently married, might possibly send her a card, and Henry, her elder brother, a solicitor and family man, wouldn't give her a thought, although his wife might possibly remember. There was Gregory, of course, with whom she had that old-fashioned thing an 'understanding'...

She got up then, wasting a few minutes hanging out of the window to admire the view; she never tired of it—rural Dorset. Away from the main roads, the village was half hidden by a small wood, the hills were close by and beyond them lay the quiet countryside. The church clock struck seven and she withdrew her head and set about getting dressed, then skimmed downstairs to the kitchen to make the early-morning tea.

The kitchen was large, with a lamentable lack of

5

up-to-date equipment. There was a scrubbed wooden table ringed around by sturdy chairs, an old-fashioned gas cooker flanking a deep sink and a vast dresser along one wall. There was a shabby rug in front of the cooker and two Windsor chairs, in one of which there was a small tabby cat to whom Serena wished a good morning before she put on the kettle. The one concession to modernity was a cumbersome fridge which, more often than not, ran amok.

Serena left the kettle to boil and went to the front door to fetch the post. There was a small pile of letters in the post box, and just for a moment she pretended that they were all for her. They weren't, of course: bills, several legal-looking envelopes, a catalogue or two, and, just as she had expected, two birthday cards for herself. And no card from Gregory. But she hadn't really expected one from him; he had made it plain to her on several occasions that birthdays were scandalously overpriced and a waste of money. Gregory didn't believe in wasting money; her father and brothers approved of him for that reason. Serena wasn't sure of that, but she hoped in a vague way that when they married she would be able to change his frugal ways.

She went back to the kitchen and made the tea, offered milk to the cat and, as the clock struck the half hour, took a tray of tea up to her father's room.

This was a large, gloomy apartment with heavy

old-fashioned furniture, closely curtained against the morning brightness. She tweaked one curtain aside as she crossed the room, the better to see the occupant in the vast bed.

Mr Lightfoot matched the room, gloomy and the epitome of a late-Victorian gentleman, whiskers and all. He sat up in bed, not speaking, and when Serena wished him good morning, he grunted a reply.

'A good morning for some,' he observed, 'but for those who suffer as I do, daylight is merely the solace after a sleepless night.'

Serena put the tray down and handed him his letters. That her father's snores shattered the peace of the house was something on which there was no point in remarking. She had long ago learned that the only way in which to live with him was to allow his words to flow over her head. She said now, 'It's my birthday, Father.'

He was opening his letters. 'Oh, yes? Why have the gas company sent me another bill? Gross carelessness.'

'Perhaps you didn't pay the first one?'

'Don't be ridiculous, Serena. I have always paid my bills promptly.'

'But it is possible to make a mistake,' said Serena, and took herself out of the room, wondering for the thousand and first time how her mother could have lived with such a tiresome man. She herself very often found life quite intolerable, living here with him, doing almost all of the housework, cooking and shopping and looking after him. He had for some time now declared that he was an invalid, and he led an invalid's life with no concern for her.

Since Dr Bowring had said that there was nothing wrong with him he had refused to see him again, declaring that he knew far better what was wrong with him than any doctor. So he had devised his own treatment for his illness, having declared that he was suffering from a weak heart and congestion of the lungs. He had over the years added lumbago to these, which gave him every reason to take to his bed whenever he wished to do so.

It hadn't been so bad when her mother had been alive. They had had a housekeeper, and between the two of them Serena and her mother had devised a routine which had allowed them enough freedom; there had been a certain amount of social life for them. Serena had had her tennis parties and small dances at friends' houses, and her mother had been able to play bridge and enjoy coffee with her friends. Then her mother had fallen ill and died without fuss or complaint, only asking Serena to look after her father. And, since Serena had known that her mother had loved her despot of a husband, she had promised that she would. That had been five years ago...

Her life since then had altered dramatically: the

housekeeper had been dismissed; Serena, her father had declared, was quite capable of running the house with the help of a woman from the village who came twice a week for a few hours. What else was there for her to do? he'd wanted to know, when she had pointed out that the house wasn't only large, it was devoid of any labour-saving devices. Sitting in his armchair by his bedroom window, wrapped in rugs, with a small table beside him bearing all the accepted aids to invalidism, he had dismissed her objections with a wave of the hand.

Since she had to account for every penny of the housekeeping allowance he gave her each month she'd had no chance to improve things. True, there was a washing machine, old now, and given to rather frightening eruptions and sinister clankings, and there was central heating in some of the rooms. But this was turned off at the end of March and not started again until October. Since the plumber from Yeovil came each half-year and turned it on and off, there wasn't much she could do about that.

Serena, recognising the brick wall she was up against, had decided sensibly to make the best of things. After all, Gregory Pratt, a junior partner in the solicitors' firm in Sherborne, had hinted on several occasions that he was considering marrying her at some future date. She liked him well enough, although she had once or twice found herself stifling a yawn when he chose to entertain her with a resumé of his day's work, but she supposed that she would get used to that in time.

When he brought her flowers, and talked vaguely about their future together, she had to admit to herself that it would be nice to marry and have a home and her own children. She wasn't in love with Gregory, but she liked him, and although like any other girl she dreamed of being swept off her feet by some magnificent man, she thought it unlikely that it would happen to her.

Her mother, when she'd been alive, had told her that she was a *jolie laide*, but her father had always been at pains to tell her that she was downright plain, an opinion upheld by her brothers, so that she had come to think of herself as just that—a round face, with a small nose and a wide mouth, dominated by large brown eyes and straight light brown hair worn long, in a rather careless knot on top of her head. That her mouth curved sweetly and her eyes had thick curling lashes was something she thought little of, nor did she consider her shape, pleasingly plump, to be much of an asset. Since Gregory had never, as far as she could remember, commented upon her appearance, there had been no one to make her think otherwise.

She went back to the kitchen and boiled an egg for her breakfast, and put her two cards on the mantelpiece. 'I am twenty-six, Puss,' she said, addressing the tabby cat, 'and since it is my birthday I shall do no housework; I shall go for a walk—up Barrow Hill.'

She finished her breakfast, tidied the kitchen, put everything ready for lunch and went to get her father's breakfast tray.

He was reading his paper and didn't look up. 'I'll have a little ham for lunch, and a few slices of thin toast. My poor appetite gives me concern, Serena, although I cannot hope that you share that concern.'

'Well, you had a splendid breakfast,' Serena pointed out cheerfully. 'Egg, bacon, toast and marmalade, and coffee. And, of course, if you got up and had a walk that would give you an appetite.'

She gave him a kindly smile; he was an old tyrant, greedy and selfish, but her mother had asked her to look after him. Besides, she felt sorry for him, for he was missing so much from life. 'I'm going out for a walk,' she told him. 'It's a lovely morning…'

'A walk? And am I to be left alone in the house?'

'Well, when I go to the shops you're alone, aren't you? The phone is by the bed, and you can get up if you want and go downstairs for a change.'

She reached the door. 'I'll be back for coffee,' she told him.

She fetched a jacket—an elderly garment she kept for gardening—found stout shoes, put a handful of biscuits into a pocket and left the house. Barrow Hill looked nearer than it was, but it was still early. She turned away from the road leading down to the village, climbed a stile and took the footpath beside a field of winter wheat.

It was a gentle climb to start with, and she didn't hurry. The trees and hedges were in leaf, there were lambs bleating and birds singing and the sky was blue, a washed-out blue, dotted with small woolly clouds. She stopped to stare up at it; it was indeed a beautiful morning, and she was glad that she had rebelled against the routine of housework and cooking. No doubt her father would be coldly angry when she got back, but nothing he could say would spoil her pleasure now.

The last bit of Barrow Hill was quite steep, along a path bordered by thick undergrowth, but presently it opened out onto rough ground covered in coarse grass and strewn with rocks, offering a splendid view of the surrounding countryside. It was a solitary spot, but she saw that today she was going to have to share it with someone else. A man was sitting very much at ease on one of the larger rocks—the one, she noticed crossly, which she considered her own.

He had turned round at the sound of her careful progress through the stones and grass tufts, and now he stood up. A very tall man, with immensely broad shoulders, wearing casual tweeds. As she went towards him she saw that he was a handsome man too, but past his first youth. Nearer forty than thirty, she reflected as she wished him good morning, casting a look at her rock as she did so.

His 'Good morning,' was cheerful. 'Am I trespassing on your rock?'

She was rather taken aback. 'Well, it's not my rock, but whenever I come up here I sit on it.'

He smiled, and she found herself smiling back. He had a nice smile and it was unexpected, for his features were forbidding in repose—a powerful nose, heavy-lidded blue eyes and a thin mouth above the decidedly firm chin. Not a man to treat lightly, she thought.

She sat down without fuss on the rock, and he sat on a tree stump some yards away. He said easily, 'I didn't expect to find anyone here. It's quite a climb...'

'Not many people come up here for that reason, and, of course, those living in the village mostly go to Yeovil to work each day. In the summer sometimes people come and picnic. Not often, though, for they can't bring a car near enough...'

'So you have it to yourself?'

She nodded. 'But I don't come as often as I would like to...'

'You work in Yeovil too?'

He asked the question so gently that she answered, 'Oh, no. I live at home.'

He glanced at her hands, lying idly in her lap. Small hands, roughened by work, not the hands of a lady of leisure. She caught his glance and said in a matter-of-fact way, 'I look after my father and run the house.'

'And you have escaped? Just for a while?'

'Well, yes. You see, it's my birthday...'

'Then I must wish you a very happy day.' When she didn't reply, he added, 'I expect you will be celebrating this evening? A party? Family?'

'No. My brothers and their families don't live very close to us.'

'Ah, well—but there is always the excitement of the postman, isn't there?'

She agreed so bleakly that he began to talk about the country around them; a gentle flow of conversation which soothed her, so that presently she was able to tell him some of the local history and point out the landmarks.

But a glance at her watch set her on her feet. 'I must go.' She smiled at him. 'I enjoyed talking to you. I do hope you will enjoy your stay here.'

He got up and wished her a pleasant goodbye, and if she had half hoped that he would suggest going back to the village with her she was disappointed.

It had been pleasant, she reflected, going hurriedly

back along the path. He had seemed like an old friend, and she suspected that she had talked too much. But that wouldn't matter; she wasn't likely to see him again. He had told her casually that he was a visitor. And now she came to think of it he hadn't sounded quite English...

She reached the house a little out of breath; her father had his coffee at eleven o'clock each morning and it was five minutes to the hour. She put the kettle on, still in her jacket, and ground the beans, then kicked off her shoes, smoothed her hair, laid a tray and, once more her quiet self, went up to her father's room.

He was sitting in his great armchair by the window, reading. He looked up as she went in. 'There you are. Gregory telephoned. He has a great deal of work. He hopes to see you at the weekend.'

'Did he wish me a happy birthday?' She put down the tray and waited hopefully.

'No. He is a busy man, Serena. I think that you sometimes forget that.' He picked up his book. 'I fancy an omelette for lunch.' He added reprovingly, 'My bed is not yet made; I shall probably need to rest after I have eaten.'

Serena went back downstairs, reminding herself that she had had a few hours of pure pleasure on Barrow Hill; it would be something to think about. She supposed that it was because it was her birthday that she had been so chatty with the stranger there. She blushed at the thought.

'Not that it matters,' she told Puss, offering the small beast sardines from the tin she had opened. 'He doesn't know me from Adam, and I don't know him, though I think he'd be rather a nice person to know. He'll have forgotten all about me…'

However, he hadn't. He walked back to Dr Bowring's house, thinking about her. He had known the doctor and his wife for many years—they had been medical students and she a nurse—creating an easy friendship which had lasted, despite the fact that he lived and worked in Holland. On his occasional visits to England he contrived to see them, although this was the first time he had visited them in Somerset. At lunch he told them of his walk up Barrow Hill.

'And I met a girl there—rather shabby clothes, round face, brown hair—very untidy, nice voice. Said she looked after her father but she'd escaped for an hour or two because it was her birthday.'

'Serena Lightfoot,' chorused his companions. 'A perfect darling,' said Mrs Bowring. 'Her father's the horridest old man I've ever met. Threw George out, didn't he, darling?'

The doctor nodded. 'He's perfectly fit, but has decided to be an invalid for the rest of his life. I'm not allowed in the house, but from what I can glean from the village gossip he spends his days sitting around or lying in bed, enjoying ill health. When his wife died he sacked the housekeeper, and now Serena runs the place with old Mrs Pike going there twice a week. No life for a girl.'

'So why doesn't she leave? She's old enough and wise enough, surely?'

'I've done my best to persuade her to get a job away from home—so has the rector—but it seems that she promised her mother that she would look after him. It's not all gloom and doom though. It's an open secret in the village that Gregory Pratt intends to marry her. He's a partner in a law firm in Sherborne. A prudent man, with an eye on Mr Lightfoot's not inconsiderable financial status and the house—both of which it is presumed he will leave to Serena. She has two brothers, both with incomes of their own and steady positions, but neither of them see much of her or their father, and have let it be known that they neither expect nor want anything when he dies.'

'So is Serena by way of being an heiress?'

'It seems so. Neither her father nor her brothers seem to have mentioned it to her, but I have heard that Gregory is aware of it.'

'So he would have told her, surely?'

'Oh, no. That might give her the idea that he only wants to marry her for her money and the house.'

The Dutchman raised heavy brows. 'And does he?'

'Of course. My dear Ivo! He's not in love with her, I feel sure, and I doubt very much if she is with him, but he's always very attentive if they should go out together, which isn't often, and I think she likes him well enough. She's a sensible girl; she knows she hasn't much in the way of looks, and very little chance of leaving home unless her father dies. Even then she has had little chance to go out into the world and meet people.'

'It's a shame,' said Mrs Bowring, 'for she's great fun and so kind and gentle; she must long for pretty clothes and a chance to meet people of her own age. You've no idea what a job it is to get her here for drinks or dinner. Her wretched father manages to feel ill at the last minute, or he telephones just as we're sitting down to dinner and demands her back home because he's dying.'

They began to talk of other things then, and Serena wasn't spoken of again. Two days later Mr van Doelen drove himself back to London and shortly after, back to Holland.

It was the following Saturday when Gregory called to see Serena, although after greeting her in a somewhat perfunctory fashion he went upstairs to see her father. A man who knew on which side his bread was buttered, and intending to have jam on it too, he lost no opportunity of keeping on good terms with Mr Lightfoot. He spent half an hour or so discussing the stockmarket, and listening with every appearance of serious attention to Mr Lightfoot's pithy remarks about the government, before going back downstairs to the sitting room to find Serena sitting on the floor, doing the *Telegraph* crossword puzzle.

He sat down in one of the old-fashioned armchairs. 'Would you not be more comfortable in a chair, Serena?'

'Do you suppose an etui is the same thing as a small workbag, Gregory?'

He frowned. 'Really, my dear, you ask the most stupid questions.'

'Well, they can't be all that stupid or they wouldn't be in a crossword puzzle.' She sat back on her heels and looked at him. 'You forgot my birthday.'

'Did I? After all, birthdays aren't important, not once one is adult.'

Serena pencilled in a word. Gregory was probably quite right; he so often was—and so tolerant. Her brothers had told her that he would be a good and kind husband. Sometimes, though, she wondered if she would have liked him to be a little more exciting. And why was it that everyone took it for granted that she would marry him?

She said now, 'I should have liked a card, and flowers—a great sheaf of roses in Cellophane tied with ribbon—and a very large bottle of perfume.'

Gregory laughed. 'You really must grow up, Serena. You must have been reading too many novels. You know my opinion about wasting money on meaningless rubbish...'

She pencilled in another word. 'Why should flowers and presents be meaningless rubbish when they are given to someone you love or want to please? Have you ever felt that you wanted to buy me something madly extravagant, Gregory?'

He lacked both imagination and a sense of humour, and besides, he had a high opinion of himself. He said seriously, 'No, I can't say that I have. What would be the point, my dear? If I were to give you a diamond necklace, or undies from Harrods, when would you have the occasion to wear them?'

'So when you buy me a present at Christmas you think first, Now, what can I buy Serena that she can find useful and use each day? Like that thing you gave me for shredding things which takes all day to clean?'

He refused to get annoyed. He gave her an indulgent smile. 'I think you must be exaggerating, Serena. How about a cup of tea? I can't stay long; I'm dining with the head of my department this evening.'

So she fetched the tea, and he told her of his

week's work while he drank it and ate several slices of the cake she had baked. Since she had little to say, and that was sensible, he reflected that despite her lack of looks she would be a quite suitable wife for him; he didn't allow himself to dwell on the house and the comfortable inheritance she would have, and which would make her even more suitable.

He went back upstairs to say goodbye to Mr Lightfoot, and presently came down again to give her a peck on a cheek and tell her that he would do his utmost to come and see her the following weekend.

Serena shut the door behind him and gathered up the tea things. She reflected that Gregory wasn't just frugal, he was downright mean. Washing up, impervious to her father's voice demanding attention, she considered Gregory. She wasn't sure when it had first become apparent that he was interested in her. She had felt flattered and prepared to like him, for her life had been dull, and, after a while, her father had signified his approval of him. When her brothers had met him, they had assured her in no uncertain terms that Gregory would be a splendid husband, and she, with the prospect of a life of her own, had allowed herself to agree with them.

But now the years were slipping away, and Gregory, although he talked often enough of when they would marry, had never actually asked her to marry him. He had a steady job, too. Serena being Serena, honest and guileless and expecting everyone else to be the same—except for her father, of course—had never for one moment thought that Gregory was waiting for her father to die, at which point he would marry her and become the owner of the house and a nice little capital. He had no doubt that Serena would be only too glad to let him take over the house and invest her money for her. He didn't intend to be dishonest, she would have all she wanted within reason, but it would be his hand which held the strings of her moneybags.

Of course, Serena knew nothing of this... All the same doubts were beginning to seep into her head. Other thoughts seeped in, too, about the stranger she had talked to so freely on Barrow Hill. She had liked him; it had seemed to her that she had known him for a long time, that he was like an old, trusted friend. Nonsense, of course—but, nonsense or not, his memory stayed clearly in her head.

During the week her elder brother came. His visits were infrequent, although he lived in Yeovil, but, as he pointed out, he was a busy man with little leisure. At Christmas and on his father's birthday he came, with his wife and two children—duty visits no one enjoyed—and every month or so he came briefly. He was very like his father, and they didn't get on well, so the visits were brief. Serena, offering coffee or tea, was always questioned closely as to finances, warned to let him know if she should ever need him, but was never asked if she was happy or content with the life she led. And this visit was like all the others: brief and businesslike with no mention of herself.

Over a second cup of coffee she said, 'I should like a holiday, Henry.'

'A holiday? Whatever for? Really, Serena, you are sometimes quite lacking in sense. You have a pleasant life here; you have friends in the village and leisure. And who is to look after Father if you were to go away?'

'You could pay someone—or your wife Alice could come and stay. You said yourself that you have a splendid au pair who could look after the children.'

Henry's colour had heightened. 'Impossible. Alice has the house to run, and quite a busy social life. Really, Serena, I had no idea that you were so selfish.' He added, 'And the au pair is leaving.'

He went away then, wishing her an austere goodbye, leaving her to go upstairs and discover why her father was shouting for her.

A few days later her younger brother came. Matthew was a gentler version of his brother. He also didn't get on well with his father, but he was a dutiful son, tolerant of Mr Lightfoot's ill temper while at the same time paying no more than duty visits. He was accompanied by his wife, a forceful young woman who was scornful of Serena, whom she considered was hopelessly old-fashioned in her ideas. She came into the house declaring breezily that Serena was neglecting the garden, and did she know there was a tile loose on the porch roof?

'These things need attention,' she pointed out. 'It doesn't do to neglect a house, certainly not one as large as this one. I must say you're very lucky to live so splendidly.'

Serena let that pass, allowing her sister-in-law's voice to flow over her unlistening head while her brother went to see his father. It was while they were having tea that she said, 'Henry came the other day. I told him I wanted a holiday.'

Matthew choked on his cake. 'A holiday? Why, Serena?'

At least he sounded reasonably interested.

'This is a large house, there are six bedrooms, attics, a drawing room, dining room, sitting room, kitchen and two bathrooms. I am expected to keep them all clean and polished with the help of an elderly woman from the village who has rheumatism and can't bend. And there's the garden. I had a birthday a week or so ago—I'm twenty-six—and I think I'm entitled to a holiday.'

Matthew looked thoughtful, but it was his wife who spoke. 'My dear Serena, we would all like holidays, but one has one's duty. After all, you have only yourself and your father to care for, and uninterrupted days in which to arrange your tasks to please yourself.'

'But I don't please myself,' said Serena matter-of-factly. 'I have to please Father.'

Matthew said, 'Well, it does seem to me to be quite reasonable… You have spoken to Henry…?'

'Yes, he thinks it's a silly idea.'

Matthew was at heart a good man, but under his brother and his wife's thumbs. He said, 'Oh, well, in that case I don't think you should think any more about it, Serena.'

When Serena said nothing, he added, 'I dare say you see a good deal of Gregory?' Then he said, 'A steady young man. You could do worse, Serena.'

'Well, I dare say I could do better,' said Serena flippantly. 'Only I never meet any other men.'

She had a sudden memory of the man on Barrow Hill.

Gregory came at the weekend. She hadn't expected him and, since it was a wet, dreary day, had decided to turn out a kitchen cupboard. Her untidy appearance caused him to frown as he pecked her cheek.

'Must you look like a drudge on a Saturday morning?' he wanted to know. 'Surely that woman who comes to clean could do the work in the kitchen?'

Serena tucked back a strand of hair behind an ear. 'She comes twice times a week for two hours. In a house this size it barely gives her time to do the kitchen and bathrooms and Hoover. I didn't expect you…'

'Obviously. I have brought you some flowers.'

He handed her daffodils wrapped in Cellophane with the air of a man conferring a diamond necklace.

Serena thanked him nicely and forebore from mentioning that there were daffodils running riot in the garden. It's the thought that counts, she reminded herself as she took off her pinny. 'I'll make some coffee. Father has had his.'

'I'll go and see him presently.' Gregory added carefully, 'Henry tells me that you want to go on holiday.'

She was filling the kettle. 'Yes. Don't you think I deserve one? Can you think of somewhere I might go? I might meet people and have fun?'

Gregory said severely, 'You are being facetious, Serena. I cannot see why you should need to go away. You have a lovely home here, with every comfort, and you can please yourself as to how you organise your days.'

She turned to look at him. He was quite serious, she decided, and if she had expected him to back her up she was to be disappointed.

'You make it sound as though I spend my days sitting in the drawing room doing nothing, but you must know that that isn't true.'

'My dear Serena, would you be happy doing that? You are a born housewife and a splendid house-keeper; you will make a good wife.' He smiled at her. 'And now how about that coffee?'

He went to see her father presently, and she began to get lunch ready. Her father had demanded devilled kidneys on toast and a glass of the claret he kept in the dining room sideboard under lock and key. If Gregory intended to stay for lunch, he would have to have scrambled eggs and soup. Perhaps he would take her out? Down to the pub in the village where one could get delicious pasties...

Wishful thinking. He came into the kitchen, saying importantly that he needed to go to the office.

'But it's Saturday...'

He gave her a tolerant look. 'Serena, I take my job seriously; if it means a few hours' extra work even on a Saturday, I do not begrudge it. I will do my best to see you next Saturday.'

'Why not tomorrow?'

His hesitation was so slight that she didn't notice it. 'I promised mother that I would go and see her— sort out her affairs for her—she finds these things puzzling.'

His mother, reflected Serena, was one of the toughest old ladies she had ever encountered, per-fectly capable of arranging her affairs to suit herself.

But she said nothing; she was sure that Gregory was a good son.

On Sunday, with the half-hope that she might see the stranger again, she walked up to the top of Barrow Hill, but there was no one there. Moreover, the early-morning brightness had clouded over and it began to rain. She went back to roast the pheasant her father had fancied for his lunch, and then spent the afternoon with Puss, listening to the radio.

While she listened she thought about her future. She couldn't alter it for the moment, for she had given her word to her mother, but there was no reason why she shouldn't try and learn some skill, something she could do at home. She was handy with her needle, but she didn't think there was much future in that; maybe she could learn how to use a computer—it seemed that was vital for any job. There were courses she could take at home, but how to get hold of a computer?

Even if she found something, where would she get the money to pay for it? She had to account for every penny of the housekeeping money her father gave her each month, and when she had asked him for an allowance so that she might buy anything she needed for herself, he had told her to buy what she needed and have the bill sent to him. But to buy toothpaste and soap and expect the shopkeeper to send a bill for such a trivial purchase really wasn't possible, so she managed to add these items to the household bills from the village shop.

Since she hardly ever went out socially, she contrived to manage with her small wardrobe. She had on one occasion actually gone to Yeovil and bought a dress and had the bill sent to her father, but it had caused such an outcry that she had never done it since. She had never been sure if the heart attack he had assured her she had given him had been genuine or not, for he had refused to have the doctor. Instead he had lain in his bed, heaping reproaches on her head every time she had entered the room. By no means a meek girl, Serena had nonetheless felt forced to believe him.

Ten days later, on a bright May morning, Mr Perkins the family solicitor called. He was a nice old man, for when her mother had died, and he had been summoned by Mr Lightfoot, he had come upon Serena in the kitchen, crying her eyes out. He had patted her on the arm and told her not to be too unhappy.

'At least your father has provided for your future,' he had reassured her. 'You need never have that worry. I should not be telling you this, but it may help a little.'

She had thanked him and thought little of it at the time, but over the years she had come to assume that at least her future was secure.

Now Mr Perkins, older and greyer, was back again, and was closeted for a long time with her father. When he came downstairs at length he looked upset, refused the coffee she offered him and drove away with no more than a brief goodbye. He had remonstrated against Mr Lightfoot's new will, but to no avail.

Serena's brothers had mentioned her wish to have a holiday to their father. They had been well meaning, but Mr Lightfoot, incensed by what he deemed to be gross ingratitude and flightiness on the part of Serena, had, in a fit of quite uncalled for rage, altered his will.

Mr Perkins came with his clerk the next day and witnessed its signature, and on the following day Mr Lightfoot had a stroke.

CHAPTER TWO

MR LIGHTFOOT'S stroke was only to be expected; a petulant man, and a bully by nature, his intolerance had led him to believe that he was always right and everyone else either wrong or stupid. High blood pressure and an unhealthy lifestyle did nothing to help this, nor did his liking for rich food. He lay in his bed for long periods, imagining that he was suffering from some serious condition and being neglected by Serena, and now the last straw, as it were, was to be laid on the camel's back: he had ordered sweetbreads for his lunch, with a rich sauce, asparagus, and baby new potatoes, to be followed by a trifle.

Serena pointed out in her usual sensible manner that the sweetbreads would be just as tasty without the sauce, and wouldn't an egg custard be better than trifle? 'And I shall have to go to the village—the butcher may not have sweetbreads. What else would you like?'

Mr Lightfoot sat up in bed, casting the newspaper from him. 'I've told you what I wish to eat. Are you so stupid that you cannot understand me?'

'Don't get excited, Father,' said Serena. 'Mrs Pike

will be here presently, and I'll go to the village. She will bring your coffee...'

While she was in the village he refused the coffee, and then, when Mrs Pike was working in the kitchen, he went downstairs and unlocked the cupboard where he kept the whisky.

Serena, back home, bade Mrs Pike goodbye and set about getting her father's lunch. She did it reluctantly, for she considered that he ate the wrong food and was wasting his life in bed, or sitting in his chair doing nothing.

'A good walk in the fresh air,' said Serena, unwrapping the sweetbreads, 'and meeting friends, playing golf or something.' Only fresh air was contrary to Mr Lightfoot's ideas of healthy living and he had no friends now.

At exactly one o'clock she bore the tray up to his room. He was sitting up in bed, propped up on his pillows reading the *Financial Times*, but he cast the paper down as she went in.

'Well, bring the tray here, Serena. How very slow you are. Probably because you don't have enough to do. I must consider dismissing Mrs Pike. There isn't enough work for two strong women to do in this house.'

Serena set the tray on his knees. She said, in the colourless voice she used when she needed to show self-restraint, 'Mrs Pike is sixty and has rheumatism;

she can't kneel or bend—you can hardly call her strong. Even if I'm strong, I have only one pair of hands. If you send her away it would mean that either I do no housework and look after you and cook, or do the housework and feed you sandwiches.'

He wasn't listening, but poking at the food on his plate with a fork.

'These aren't lamb's sweetbreads. I particularly told you that they are the only ones I am able to digest.'

'The butcher only had these…'

Mr Lightfoot raised his voice to a roar. 'You thoughtless girl. You are quite uncaring of my comfort and health.'

He picked up the plate and threw it across the room, and a second later had his stroke.

'Father,' said Serena urgently, and when he lay silently against his pillows she sped to the bed. Her father was a nasty colour and he was breathing noisily, his eyes closed. She took his pulse, settled his head more comfortably on a pillow and reached for the phone by the bed.

Dr Bowring, on the point of carving the half-leg of lamb his wife had set before him, put down the carving knife as the phone rang.

He addressed his wife and their guest in a vexed

voice. 'This always happens just as we are about to have a meal. Sorry about this, Ivo.'

He went to answer the phone, and was back again within a minute.

'Serena Lightfoot. Her father has collapsed. He isn't my patient. He showed me the door a couple of years ago; doesn't believe in doctors, treats himself and has turned into a professional invalid. But I'll have to go...' He glanced at Ivo van Doelen. 'Like to come with me, Ivo? She's alone, and if he's fallen I'll need help.'

Serena, shocked though she was, didn't lose her head. She ran downstairs and opened the front door, and then went back to her father. She had little idea as to what to do for him, so she sat on the side of the bed and took one of his flaccid hands in hers and told him in a quiet voice that he wasn't to worry, that the doctor was coming, that he would be better presently; she had read somewhere or other that quite often someone who had had a stroke was able to hear, even if they were unable to speak...

The two men came quietly into the room and saw her sitting there. They saw the mess of asparagus, potatoes and sweetbreads too, scattered on the floor. Dr Bowring said quietly, 'Hello, Serena. You don't mind that I have brought a friend—a medical man, too—with me? I wasn't sure if there would be any lifting to do.'

She nodded, and looked in a bewildered fashion at his companion. It was the man who had been on Barrow Hill. She got up from the bed to make way for the two men.

'Can you tell me what happened?'

She told him in a quiet voice, and added, 'You see, he was angry because they weren't the sweetbreads he had told me to get. The butcher didn't have them.' She sighed. 'I annoyed him, and now he's really ill…'

'No, Serena, it has nothing to do with you. Your father, while I was allowed to attend to him, had a very high blood pressure; neglect of that condition made a stroke inevitable. You have no reason to reproach yourself. Perhaps you would like to make yourself a cup of tea; we shan't be long.'

So she went down to the kitchen, made a pot of tea and sat at the kitchen table drinking it, for there was nothing else for her to do until Dr Bowring came downstairs.

When he did he sat down at the table opposite her. 'You don't mind Mr van Doelen being here?'

She glanced at the big man, who was leaning against the dresser. 'No, no, of course not…'

'Your father has had a severe stroke. He is too ill for him to be moved to hospital, I'm afraid. In fact, my dear, I believe that he will not recover. I'll get the community nurse to come as soon as possible. If necessary she will stay the night. Presumably your brothers will come as soon as possible and see to things?'

'I'll telephone them. Thank you for coming, Dr Bowring.'

'I'll come in the morning, or sooner if you need me. If by any chance I'm on another case, will you allow Mr van Doelen to come in my place?'

She glanced at the big man, standing so quietly, saying nothing and yet somehow making her feel safe. 'No, of course I don't mind.'

'Then if I may use your phone to get Nurse Sims up here. Until she comes I'm sure Dr van Doelen will stay with you.'

'Oh, but I'll be all right.' She knew that it was a silly thing to say as soon as she had uttered the words, so she added, 'Thank you, that would be very kind.'

Dr Bowring went presently, and Mr van Doelen, with a reassuring murmur, went upstairs to her father's room. Presently Nurse Sims came, and he bade Serena a quiet goodbye after talking to Nurse Sims.

Serena had phoned her brothers; they would come as soon as possible, they had both told her. She sensed that they found her father's illness an inconvenience, but then illness never took convenience into account, did it? She set about getting a room ready for Nurse Sims, and getting the tea. She had gone upstairs to see her father, but he was still unconscious and she could see that he was very ill. Nurse Sims had drawn a comfortable chair up to the bed and was knitting placidly.

'There's nothing for me to do. It's just a question of waiting. Are your brothers coming?'

'As soon as possible, they said. Is there anything I can do?'

'No, Serena. Go and have a cup of tea. I'll have mine here, if you don't mind…'

Henry arrived first, and went at once to see his father, then accepted the cup of tea Serena offered him before going away to see Dr Bowring. He was closely followed by Matthew, who stayed with his father for some time and then came down to sit with Serena, not saying much until Henry returned.

Neither of them would be able to stay. Henry explained pompously that he had important work to do, and Matthew had his parochial duties. She was to telephone them immediately if their father's condition worsened. She would be companioned throughout the night by the nurse, and in the morning they would review the situation.

'It is impossible for Alice to come,' Henry pointed out. 'She has the children and the house to run.' And Matthew regretted that his wife Norah had the

Mother's Union and various other parish duties to fulfill.

Serena bade them goodbye and went into the kitchen to see about supper. She wasn't upset; she hadn't expected either of them to offer any real help. They had left her to manage as best she could for years, and there was no reason to expect them to do otherwise now.

She got supper, relieved Nurse Sims while she ate hers, and then got ready for bed and went and sat with her father while Nurse Sims took a nap. Since there was nothing to be done for the moment, presently she went to her own bed.

She was in the kitchen making tea at six o'clock the next morning when Nurse Sims asked her to phone the doctor.

It was Mr Van Doelen who came quietly into the kitchen. 'Dr Bowring is out on a baby case. Shall I go up?'

Serena gave him a tired 'Hello.' She was both tired and very worried, her hair hanging down her back in a brown cloud, her face pale. She was wrapped in an elderly dressing gown and she had shivered a little in the early-morning air as he had opened the door. She led the way upstairs and stood quietly while he and Nurse Sims bent over her father. Presently he straightened up.

He said gently, 'Would you like to stay with your

father? It won't be very long, I'm afraid.' When she nodded, he drew up a chair for her. 'I'll sit over here, if I may?' He moved to the other end of the room. 'I'm sure Nurse Sims would like a little rest?'

Mr Lightfoot died without regaining consciousness; Serena, sitting there holding his hand, bade him a silent farewell. He had never liked her, and she, although she had looked after him carefully, had long ago lost any affection she had had for him. All the same, she was sad…

Mr van Doelen eased her gently out of her chair. 'If you would fetch Nurse Sims? And perhaps telephone your brothers? And I'm sure we could all do with a cup of tea.'

He stayed until her brothers came, dealt with Henry's officious requests and questions, and then bade her a quiet goodbye. 'Dr Bowring will be along presently,' he told her, 'and I'm sure your brothers will see to everything.'

She saw him go with regret.

The next few days didn't seem quite real. Henry spent a good deal of time at the house, sorting out his father's papers, leaving her lists of things which had to be done.

'You'll need to be kept busy,' he told her, and indeed she was busy, for the writing of notes to her father's few friends, preparing for their arrival and the meal they would expect after the funeral fell to her lot, on top of the usual housekeeping and the extra meals Henry expected while he was there. Not that she minded; she was in a kind of limbo. Her dull life had come to an end but the future was as yet unknown.

At least, not quite unknown. Gregory had come to see her when he had heard the news and, while he didn't actually propose, he had let her see that he considered their future together was a foregone conclusion. And he had been kind, treating her rather as though she were an invalid, telling her that she had always been a dutiful daughter and now she would have her reward. She hadn't been listening, otherwise she might have wondered what he was talking about.

Not many people came to the funeral, and when the last of them had gone old Mr Perkins led the way into the drawing room. Henry and Matthew and their wives made themselves comfortable with the air of people expecting nothing but good news. Serena, who didn't expect anything, sat in the little armchair her mother had always used.

Mr Perkins cleaned his spectacles, cleared his throat and began to read. Mr Lightfoot had left modest sums to his sons, and from the affronted look with which this was received it was apparent that, despite the fact that they had expected nothing, they were disappointed.

'The house and its contents,' went on Mr Perkins

in a dry-as-dust voice, 'are bequeathed to a charity, to be used as a home for those in need.' He coughed. 'To Serena, a sum of five hundred pounds has been left, and here I quote: "She is a strong and capable young woman, who is quite able to make her own way in the world without the aid of my money". I must add that I did my best to persuade your father to reconsider this will, but he was adamant.'

He went presently, after assuring them that he was at their service should he be needed, and taking Serena aside to tell her that he would see that she had a cheque as soon as possible. 'And if I can help in any way...'

She thanked him, kissing his elderly cheek. 'I'll be all right,' she assured him. 'I don't need to move out at once, do I?'

'No, no. It will be several weeks before the necessary paperwork can be done.'

'Oh, good. Time for me to make plans.' She smiled at him so cheerfully that he went away easier in his mind.

Serena went back to the drawing room. Her brothers were discussing their inheritance, weighing the pros and cons of investments, while their wives interrupted with suggestions that the money would be better spent on refurbishing their homes and wardrobes. They broke off their discussions when she joined them, and Henry said gravely that of course the money would be put to good use.

'I have heavy commitments,' he pointed out, 'and the children to educate.' That they were at state schools and not costing him a penny was neither here nor there. Serena could see that he was anxious to impress upon her that she couldn't expect any financial help from him.

It was Matthew who asked her what she intended to do. 'For I am surprised at Father leaving you so ill provided for. Perhaps we could—?'

His wife interrupted smoothly, 'Serena is bound to find a good job easily; such a practical and sensible girl, and only herself to worry about. I must admit that I—we are very relieved to have inherited something. It will be just enough to have central heating put in—the house is so damp...'

'I thought the Church Council, or whatever it is, paid for things like that,' said Serena.

Her sister-in-law went red. 'We might have to wait for months—years, even—while they decide to have it done.' She added sharply, 'Matthew's income is very small.'

Serena reflected that Matthew had a private income from a legacy both brothers had received from an old aunt years ago. Neither of them needed to worry about money, but there was no point in reminding them of that! She offered coffee and sandwiches and presently bade them goodbye. They would keep in touch, they told her as they drove away.

She cleared away the cups and saucers and plates, fed Puss and sat down to have a think about her future. She was a practical girl, and for the moment she put aside her own vague plans. They were to be allowed to take personal property and gifts before the house was handed over, and the house would need to be left in good order. She would need to get the cases and trunks down from the attic so that their possessions could be packed. There were bills to be paid too, and people to notify. Only when that was done could she decide what she would do.

At the back of her mind, of course, was the reluctant thought that Gregory might want to marry her. It was an easy solution for her future but, tempting though it was to have the rest of her life settled without effort on her part, she was doubtful. It was, of course, the sensible thing to do, but under her practical manner there was the hope, romantic and deeply buried, that one day she would meet a man who would love her as dearly as she would him. And that man *wasn't* Gregory.

She went to bed presently, with Puss for company, and since it had been a busy and rather sad day, she went immediately to sleep.

Gregory had been at the funeral, but he hadn't

come to the house afterwards, pleading an appointment he had been unable to cancel. He would come, he had assured her, on the following evening.

'We have a great deal to talk about,' he had told her, smiling and looking at her with what she'd decided was a proprietary look.

She hadn't minded that, for yesterday she had been feeling in need of cherishing. Now, in the cold light of early morning, common sense took over. Gregory might not be the man of her dreams, but if he loved her she might in time learn to love him, too. She liked him, was even a little fond of him, but she had the wit to know that that was because she hadn't had the opportunity to meet other men...

She spent the day busily, dragging down cases and a trunk from the attics, clearing out her father's bedroom, and, after a sandwich and coffee, sitting down to write letters to those who had written and sent flowers. She had tea then, and changed into a sweater and skirt, did her hair and face and put a tray ready with coffee. She lighted a small fire in the sitting room, for the evening was chilly, and sat down to wait for Gregory.

He was late. His car wouldn't start, he explained, adding that he would soon be able to get a new one. He smiled as he said it, but Serena, pouring the coffee, didn't see that.

They talked for a little while about the funeral,

until he put down his cup, saying, 'Well, Serena, there's no reason why we shouldn't get married as soon as we can arrange it. I'll move in here, of course. I've always liked this house. We can modernise it a little—perhaps another bathroom, have the central heating updated, have the rooms redecorated.' He smiled at her. 'We must use your money to its best advantage, and you can rely on me getting the best advice as to investing your capital…'

Serena had been pouring herself another cup of coffee. She put the pot down carefully. 'But this house isn't mine.' She sounded quite matter-of-fact about it. 'Father has left it to charity.'

Gregory said sharply, 'But he has left you a legacy? He was comfortably off, you know.'

'Five hundred pounds,' said Serena, still very matter-of-fact. 'The rest goes with the house.'

'But this is preposterous. You must contest the will. What about your brothers?' Gregory wasn't only surprised, he was angry. 'And how are you supposed to live? Something must be done about it at once.'

'I don't see why,' said Serena in a reasonable voice. 'If this is what Father wanted, why change it? Henry and Matthew are quite happy about it.' She paused. 'And if you're going to marry me, I don't need to worry, do I?'

Gregory went red. 'You must see that this alters

all my plans, Serena. I'm an ambitious man and I need a secure background, a good living standard, a suitable house…'

'What you mean is that you need to marry a well-to-do girl. Not me.'

Gregory looked relieved. 'What a sensible girl you are, Serena. You understand me…'

Serena stood up. 'Oh, I do, Gregory, and nothing would make me marry you if you were the last man living. Now, will you go away? I don't want to see you again, and now I come to think about it, I wouldn't like to be married to you. Run along and find that rich girl!'

Gregory started towards her. 'Let us part…' he began.

'Oh, do go along,' said Serena.

After he had gone she went to the kitchen to get her supper—scrambled eggs on toast—and, since she felt that this was something of an occasion, she took the keys of the sideboard and chose a bottle of claret.

She ate at the kitchen table, with Puss at her feet enjoying a treat from a tin of sardines. And she drank two glasses of claret. She supposed that she would have been feeling unhappy and worried, but she was pleased to discover that all she felt was relief. She had five hundred pounds and the world before her in which to find the man of her dreams. She tossed back the last of the claret in her glass.

There was no need to look for him. She had already found him, although she wasn't sure if a brief acquaintance with Dr van Doelen was sufficient to clinch the matter. She thought not. Indeed, it was unlikely that their paths would cross in the future. She would do better to get herself a job and hope to meet a man as like him as possible.

Nicely buoyed up, she by the claret and Puss by an excess of sardines, they went upstairs to bed and slept dreamlessly.

Henry came in the morning, telling her importantly that he had taken a few hours off in order to look round the house and claim anything to which he was entitled. Which turned out to be quite a lot: the table silver, a claret jug and three spirit bottles in a metal frame, and the best part of a Spoke tea service which had belonged to their mother, that Matthew would have no use for nor would Serena, Henry pointed out.

'But I have no doubt that Matthew will be glad to have the dinner service. Father bought it from Selfridges, I believe, so anything which may break can be replaced. There's the new coffee percolator, too; I'll leave that for him. Where is the Wedgwood biscuit barrel, Serena?'

'In the cupboard in the dining room, Henry. Shouldn't you wait and see what Matthew wants— and what I might want?'

'My dear girl, Matthew will want useful things

which he can use in his home. Remember that he is, after all, living in a very small house, and has no social life worth mentioning.'

'But he will have when he gets a parish of his own…'

Henry ignored that. 'And you—you won't want to be lumbered with a number of useless things.'

'I don't know why you say that, Henry. You have no idea what I am going to do or where I'm going. You don't want to know, do you? Do you know that Gregory has jilted me? Or perhaps I should say he jilted my five hundred pounds.' She added bleakly, 'I thought he wanted to marry me, but all he wanted was this house and the money he thought Father would be sure to leave me.'

Henry looked uncomfortable. 'You must understand, Serena, that Gregory has his way to make in the world.'

'And what about me?'

'You're quite able to find a good job and do very well. You might even marry.'

Serena picked up a fairing from the side-table in the drawing room, where Henry was inspecting the contents of a china cabinet. The fairing was small, a man and woman holding hands, crudely done, yet charming. The kind of thing Henry and Matthew would find worthless. She would keep it for herself, a reminder of her home in happier days when her mother had been alive.

Henry bore away what he considered to be his; he had written a list of various other things, too. Serena hoped that Matthew wouldn't wait too long before making his own choice. Henry was obviously going to exert his rights as elder son.

Matthew came the next day, bringing his wife with him. The dinner service was packed up, as was an early-morning teaset which hadn't been used since their mother died. To these were added two bed-spreads, a quantity of bedlinen, the cushions from the drawing room and, at the last moment, the rather ugly clock on the mantelpiece.

'We shall probably be back,' said Matthew's wife as they left.

'My turn,' said Serena to Puss, and went slowly from room to room. She would take only small things that would go in her case or the trunk: her mother's workbox, family photographs, two china figurines to keep the fairing company, a little watercolour of the house her mother had painted. She tried to be sen-sible and think of things which would be of use to her in the future. The silver-framed travelling clock which had stood on the table by her father's bed, writing paper and pens, the cat basket from the at-tic—for of course Puss would go with her.

But where would she go? Mr Perkins had told her

that she would be able to stay at the house for two or three weeks. Tomorrow, she decided, she would go to Yeovil and go to as many employment agencies as possible.

Without much success, as it turned out. She had no qualifications, and she couldn't type, the computer was a mystery to her, and the salesladies asked for had to be experienced. She was told, kindly enough, to leave her phone number, and that if anything suitable turned up she would be notified.

But nothing turned up. The charity, anxious to take possession, were kind enough to let her stay for an extra week, and at the end of that week, still with no job in sight, Serena, Puss, her trunk and a large case, moved unwillingly into Henry's house.

Just as unwillingly she was welcomed there. There was room enough for her, for Henry lived in a large house on the outskirts of the town, but, while he wasn't slow to confide his generosity towards his sister to his colleagues, his wife made no bones in letting Serena see that she was a necessary evil. It was bad enough having her, her sister-in-law pointed out in the privacy of their bedroom, but to have to give house room to a cat as well...

As for Serena, she redoubled her efforts to find some sort of job. Housekeepers were in demand, and that was something she could do, but she wasn't going to part with Puss, and no one, it seemed, was prepared to accept a cat, especially when the applicant had no references from previous employers.

Between fruitless visits to Yeovil, she was given no chance to be idle. Her sister-in-law, a social climber by nature, quickly saw her opportunity to widen her social life, since Serena was so conveniently on hand to do the shopping and prepare meals. And when the children came home from school there was no reason, since she had nothing better to do, why she shouldn't give them their tea and keep an eye on them while they did their homework.

Serena, gritting her splendid teeth, accepted the role of unpaid domestic and put up with the childish rudeness of her nephew and niece and her brother's pompous charity. His wife's ill-concealed contempt was harder to bear, but since she was out a good deal Serena was almost able to ignore it.

She had been living with her brother for more than a week when one morning, as she was washing the breakfast dishes, alone in the house, there was a ring on the doorbell. She didn't stop to dry her hands; it was possibly the postman—probably with the answer to two more jobs she had applied for. Perhaps her luck had changed at last...

It wasn't the postman. It was Dr Bowring on the doorstep.

'I had to come to Yeovil,' he told her smilingly. 'I thought I'd just see how you were getting on.' He glanced at her wet hands and pinny. 'Is Mrs Light-foot at home?'

'No, just me. Do come in. How nice to see you. If you don't mind coming into the kitchen, I'm sure no one will mind if I make coffee.'

He looked at her enquiringly. 'No job yet?'

'Well, no. You see, I must have Puss with me, and so far no one will have her...'

He followed her into the kitchen. 'What kind of job?'

'Housekeeper or companion. I can't do anything else.' She spoke lightly, but he noted her rather pale face and the shadows under her eyes.

He said bluntly, 'You're not happy here?'

She put the instant coffee into two mugs. 'Well, it's not really convenient for Henry to have me here, and they don't like Puss.' She smiled. 'But something will turn up.'

He stayed for a little while, vaguely troubled about her, deciding silently that he would keep an eye open for a job which would suit her. It was obvious that she was unhappy, although she had made light of it.

He told his wife about her when he got back home.

'All we can do is keep our eyes open for a job for her,' said Mrs Bowring, 'and we shall have to go carefully; Serena is proud in the best sense, and she would hate to be pitied.'

* * *

Mr van Doelen had spent a busy day at one of the London hospitals; he was an orthopaedic surgeon of some repute and had come to assist at a complicated operation on a boy's shattered legs. It had been successful, and he was free to return to Holland that evening, but, leaving the hospital early that lovely summer evening, he decided against driving up to Harwich and instead picked up the car phone and dialled Dr Bowring.

Of course he was to come and spend the night— as many nights as he could spare. 'We'll wait dinner for you,' said Mrs Bowring. 'It's only four o'clock; you'll be with us in a couple of hours.'

Once free of the London suburbs, the traffic thinned and he sent the Bentley powering ahead. The countryside was bathed in sunshine, green and pleasant and exactly what he needed after hours in an operating theatre. And he need not return until the evening ferry on the following day; he had expected to be away for two days, but the operation had gone better than they had expected.

It would be good to see his friends again. He wondered idly how that girl whose father had died was getting on. She was probably married by now, to the man Mrs Bowring didn't like... Mr van Doelen had thought about her frequently, due, he considered, to the unusual circumstances of their meeting. He must remember to ask about her...

He was warmly welcomed, and Mrs Bowring went away to put the flowers he had brought into a vase while he and the doctor sat over a drink. They always found plenty to talk about and dinner was a leisurely meal. It wasn't until the men had washed up and they were all sitting in the drawing room that Mr van Doelen asked about Serena.

'You remember her?' asked Mrs Bowring. 'Such a dear girl; how that brother of hers could treat her so shabbily is beyond me.'

'Did she not intend to marry? You mentioned that…'

George Bowring explained. 'Her father left the house and almost all his money to a charity. Serena had a few weeks of leave before they took over— it's to be a home for the elderly and impoverished. He left the two sons quite adequate legacies, so I'm told, and five hundred pounds to Serena. With the observation that she was young enough and strong enough to look after herself.

'And if that wasn't bad enough, Gregory Pratt, who had let it be known that he intended to marry her, changed his mind as soon as he discovered that she hadn't inherited the house and the money. She's been trying to find work, but she refuses to abandon her cat and it's hard to find employment with no references and no skills except that of a housewife. She's living with Henry, her elder brother, at Yeovil.

I went to see her and I must say that I'm not at all happy about her. She said very little but I fancy she's having to work hard for her keep. Her sister-in-law doesn't like her overmuch, and of course Henry is a pompous ass.'

Mr van Doelen said slowly, 'It just so happens that I know of someone who is anxious to find a companion-governess for her daughter. It's the mother of the boy whom I operated on today. She plans to stay in London until the boy is fit to go home—six weeks or so. Her husband travels a good deal on business, and there is a daughter, thirteen or fourteen, living at home—Penn, near Beaconsfield, is it not? She goes to school there. There's a housekeeper and daily help, but it seems the girl is difficult to control and jealous of her brother. Would you give Miss Lightfoot a reference if they are interested? Would you like me to talk to Mrs Webster about it and see what she says? And would Miss Lightfoot be prepared to take on the job?'

'I'm sure she would, provided that she can have her cat...'

'They are extremely anxious to get someone. I should imagine that Miss Lightfoot could take any animal with her provided that she was suitable. Anyway, I'll see Mrs Webster about the boy tomorrow and let you know. It's a temporary post, but it would give her time to find her feet.'

He went back to London early the next day and, true to his promise, told Mrs Webster about Serena. 'I have met her,' he said. 'She seems a very sensible and level-headed young lady. Her one stipulation is that she may have her cat with her.'

Mrs Webster was profuse in her thanks. 'I'll drive down tomorrow and see her. She can come at once?'

'I believe so.'

Before he left London he phoned George Bowring and then wrote a letter—Miss Lightfoot needed to be told, and George might not have the time…

CHAPTER THREE

HENRY, looking up briefly as Serena put a plate of bacon and eggs before him, said, 'You'll see to the children's breakfast, will you, Serena? Alice will be down later.' He sorted through the post by his plate. 'There is a letter for you. Let us hope that it is an offer of work.'

'Let's hope it is,' agreed Serena pleasantly. She put the letter in her pocket and presently, boiling eggs for the children's breakfast, she had a look at it. The writing on the envelope was a firm and almost illegible scrawl, but there wasn't time to read the letter. It wasn't until Henry had gone and the children had been seen off to school that she sat down at the table, surrounded by breakfast debris, and opened the envelope.

The letter was short and businesslike; she read it through and then read it again. Mr van Doelen clearly had no time for the niceties of correspondence, but the facts were clear enough, and the one fact that Mrs Webster would be coming to see her that very morning with a view to engaging her as a companion for her daughter stood out like a flaming beacon. At ten o'clock, too. Serena looked at the clock; it was just after nine.

She got up, shut the door on the breakfast chaos, and went to her room, where she changed into a cotton dress, its blue rather faded but still a likely garment for a companion to wear. She powdered her nose, applied lipstick and brushed her hair into a neat coil, dusted off her sandals and went downstairs to put on the coffee pot and set a tray with cups and saucers. There had been no sound from Alice; hopefully she would sleep for another hour or two, though the doorbell might wake her.

Serena went into the hall and stood patiently by the door until, a few minutes before ten o'clock, a car stopped in front of the house.

Serena had the door open as Mrs Webster reached it. She was a tall, handsome woman, with a discontented face, expertly made up. She was well dressed, and looked as though she was used to having her own way. She paused on the porch. 'Miss Lightfoot? I'm Mrs Webster. You have been told that I would be coming to see you?'

'Yes, I had a letter. Please come in.'

Mrs Webster sat down in the drawing room and looked around her. 'I understand that you live with your brother? You have no ties? There would be no delay were I to engage you?'

'None at all, Mrs Webster. Would you like coffee?'

'Thank you. I left London quite early and I must return as soon as possible. Do you know that my son is in hospital?'

'Yes. Mr van Doelen has given me the brief facts. I'll fetch the coffee before we talk, shall I?'

Mrs Webster wasted no time. She drank her coffee quickly while she explained what she wanted. 'Heather is a wilful child, given to moods. My housekeeper is quite unable to cope with her, and I can't have her with me in London—in any case, she mustn't miss school. I shall want you to take complete charge of her until my son is able to come home. Six weeks or so, they say. My husband is away a great deal and I shall stay at a hotel so that I can visit Timothy each day. You won't have a great deal of free time, but I don't expect you to do any housework or cooking. Can you drive? Yes? There is a small car for you to use if you wish. I want you to come immediately—tomorrow, if possible. I'll send a car for you and you can go straight to Penn from here. You will be paid weekly.'

She mentioned a sum which sent Serena's spirits soaring.

'I'm offering you the post on trust; I have telephoned a Dr Bowring, who vouches for you, and, of course, Mr van Doelen's recommendation is really sufficient...'

But he hardly knows me, thought Serena, agreeing pleasantly to be ready to go to Penn on the following morning. She had no idea what the job would be like, but anything would be better than the grudging hospitality Henry and Alice were offering. Besides, she would be paid, and she could save every penny...

Mrs Webster, having got what she wanted, was disposed to be gracious. 'I'm told that you have a cat. I have no objection to you having it at Penn. I understand that you wouldn't consider going anywhere without it.' She prepared to leave. 'I shall probably see you from time to time.'

She got into her car and drove away, and Serena carried the coffee tray into the kitchen, where Puss sat uneasily in her basket. She spent her days there, aware that she was as unwelcome as Serena.

'Our luck's changed,' Serena told her. 'We're off tomorrow morning. I expect you'll be able to go where you like in the house and garden, Puss. It won't be for long, but if they like us, we'll be able to stay...'

She went upstairs to the box room, got her trunk and case and carried them into her bedroom. She hadn't unpacked everything in the trunk, and now she put it on the bed and lifted the lid. She was opening the suitcase when Alice came in, still in her dressing gown and half awake.

'What are you doing?' she demanded. 'Go and make me a cup of tea; I can't possibly get up until I've had something. I should have thought you would have come to see how I was…'

'Henry told me not to disturb you. And I'm packing—I'm going to a job tomorrow morning. I'm being fetched at nine o'clock.'

'A job? Where? Does Henry know, and why wasn't I told?'

'Henry doesn't know, and I only knew myself this morning, after he'd gone.'

'But who is to take your place? How can I manage on my own? You can't go, Serena.' She added angrily, 'How ungrateful can you be? Living here without it costing you a penny, treated like one of the family…'

'Well, I am one of the family,' Serena reminded her. 'But I can't say that I've been treated as such. I haven't much liked being a poor relation. I should have thought that you would have been glad to see the back of me.'

'I suppose I shall have to make my own tea.' Alice went away, banging the door behind her; Serena heard her squawk of rage when she opened the dining room door and saw the breakfast table.

She went downstairs presently and found Alice in

the kitchen, sitting at the table. She had a pot a tea in front of her and a plate of toast.

'You'll have to clear the dining room and kitchen,' she told Serena.

'When you're dressed we'll do it together,' said Serena briskly, and she fetched a mug and poured herself some tea and sat down opposite her sister-in-law. 'You're glad I'm going, Alice,' she observed quietly. 'I've not been welcome here; you've made that very obvious.'

'I'll be glad to see the back of you and that cat of yours. If I had my way you'd be out of the door as soon as you've packed your things.'

Serena sighed. She had tried hard to like Alice and be grateful to Henry. She took her mug to the sink. 'I'll clean the vegetables,' she said. 'By the time you've dressed I'll be ready to help you with the dining room.'

They worked silently together, and when the last plate was washed Alice threw the teacloth down by the sink. 'I'm going out to lunch. Give the children their tea when they come in.'

Serena finished her packing, made a cheese sandwich for her lunch and washed her hair, and all the time she wondered why Mr van Doelen had been the means of finding her a job, and how he had known she was in need of work. And that reminded her that she must let Dr Bowring know that she was leaving.

He might not be home, but Mrs Bowring would tell him…

He was home, on the point of leaving for his surgery. When she told him he said worriedly, 'Oh, Lord, Ivo phoned me and asked me to tell you about this job—I clean forgot. I'm so sorry, Serena.'

'It doesn't matter. He wrote to me and Mrs Webster came to see me. I'm going in the morning. I'm very grateful to him, though how he knew that I wanted a job is beyond me.'

Dr Bowring said, 'I believe that I mentioned it last time I saw him. I must go, Serena. Write and let us know how things are…and good luck!'

Which was more than Henry wished her when he got home that evening. 'I am amazed,' he said, at his most pompous. 'After all we have done for you—the ingratitude…'

Serena said matter-of-factly, 'Don't be silly, Henry. You know as well as I do that you're glad to see the back of me. I know it means you'll have to pay for another au pair, but you can afford that, can't you?'

'I don't know what Matthew will have to say to this,' began Henry.

'Why, he'll be just as relieved as you are. Only he'll be pleased that I've got a job and can start living my own life.'

She was fetched in the morning by an elderly man

in a cloth cap, driving an equally elderly car. He had a rugged, cheerful face, and explained that he was Mr Webster's gardener and handyman as he stowed her luggage in the boot. There was no one to see her go. Henry had bidden her an unforgiving goodbye when he'd left for work, the children were uncaring whether she was there or not and Alice was still in bed. Henry had made much of the fact that Alice was feeling very poorly and could scarcely lift her head off the pillow.

Serena got into the car beside the elderly man and didn't look back as he drove away.

His name, he told her, was Bob, and he'd been with the Websters for a number of years. 'Live in a cottage near the house with me wife. She cooks and housekeeps and that…there's a girl comes in each day to give an 'and.'

'It must be quite a big house,' said Serena, anxious to find out all she could before she got there.

'Middlin' big. Nice big garden. That your cat in the basket?'

'Yes. Mrs Webster said that I might have her with me. I hope your wife won't object?'

'Lor', no. Likes animals. Miss Heather'll be pleased. Always wanted a dog or cat, but Mrs Webster don't approve of them in the 'ouse.'

Serena said uneasily, 'But Puss isn't used to living

out of doors. Mrs Webster had no objection when I asked her.'

He gave a chuckle. 'Don't you worry, miss. She were that anxious to find someone to stay with Miss Heather she'd 'ave put up with a herd of elephants. See, it's like this. Master Timothy's the apple of 'is mum's eye—'is dad's too, for that matter—and Miss Heather, well, she's difficult. 'Ad her nose put out of joint when the boy was born and no one has bothered to put it straight.'

'Poor child. Thank you for telling me; it will be a great help.' She longed to ask more questions about the Websters, but it seemed prudent not to do so. Instead she asked him to tell her something about ·Penn.

The house was on the edge of the village, a white-walled gentleman's residence of some size, with green-shuttered windows and a wrought-iron balcony, surrounded by a large and beautifully kept garden.

'What gorgeous flowers, and such a lovely lawn,' said Serena, which pleased Bob.

'Mrs Webster, she doesn't care much for gardens; let's me 'ave a free 'and.'

'Oh—and Mr Webster? Doesn't he like gardens either?'

They were standing by the car before the door, looking around them.

''E's hardly ever home. Come on in, miss; Maisie'll 'ave coffee ready.'

Maisie was small and stout and placid. She welcomed Serena warmly and led the way to the kitchen. 'If you don't mind having coffee with us, miss? Your room's ready, and I thought you might like to use the little sitting room—there's a door to the garden for your cat. When Mrs Webster's away we shut up the drawing room and the dining room.'

She pulled out a chair at the kitchen table and Serena sat down. The room was large and very well equipped; no expense had been spared and everything gleamed and shone. The coffee was delicious and hot and there were slices of home-made cake to go with it. The three of them sat comfortably talking until Maisie said, 'You'll want to see your room, miss. Bob's taken your things up, and you'll have plenty of time to settle in before Heather comes back from school. She's been eating with us, but now you're here she can have her meals with you in the sitting room.'

'Oh, but won't that give you a lot of extra work?'

'To tell you the truth, miss, me and Bob will like to be on our own.'

She led Serena, with Puss in her basket, up the staircase and along a corridor at the back of the house. The room was small, but nicely furnished, and there was a small balcony overlooking the garden.

'There's no reason why you shouldn't have your little cat up here, miss, there being a balcony.'

Serena thanked her and Maisie went away, saying that they would be downstairs when she was ready to come down.

The small sitting room which Serena and Heather were to use was plainly furnished and obviously not often used. A few flowers, thought Serena, and a cushion or two, a few books lying about and Puss sitting there and it would look cosier.

She was glad to see that the garden was enclosed by a high wall so that Puss could safely roam. Lunch would be at one o'clock, and until then she was free to explore the house and the garden. The house could come later, she decided, and went into the garden with a cautious Puss. It was beautifully kept, with trim lawns and weedless flowerbeds, and away from the house there was a small summer house beside a pool filled with goldfish. A very nice garden, she considered, but it didn't look as though anyone enjoyed it much; it was all too perfect. She found a swimming pool too, tucked away behind a high hedge…

Called to have her lunch presently, she persuaded Maisie to let her share it with them in the kitchen. 'Because I know nothing about Heather—Mrs Webster was anxious to get back to her son and there was really no time. Is her school far from here? And does she have tea when she gets home? And when does she go to bed? And her friends? Do they come here sometimes?' She smiled. 'An awful lot of questions, I'm afraid.'

'Well, she's thirteen, and independent-like,' said Maisie. 'Likes her own way, too. Never has her friends here, spends a lot of time just mooning around. Got a telly of her own, and a radio...'

'She's lonely?'

'Yes, miss. Always has been. Wanted a dog or a cat, but Mrs Webster didn't want the bother.'

Serena was in the garden with Puss when Heather came home from school. She watched the girl coming towards her, a thin child, with untidy hair and a pale face which one day would be pretty but which scowled now.

'Hello,' said Serena, ignoring the scowl. 'Shall we sit here for a bit, or do you want tea straight away?'

Heather stood in front of her, staring. 'I'll have my tea when I like.'

'Right, but don't shout, Heather, or you'll frighten Puss.'

And Puss, as if on cue, poked a furry head round a nearby bush.

'You've got a cat. Mother let you have a cat here? She said I couldn't have one; it would be a nuisance.' The scowl had gone.

'Well, perhaps when she finds out how good Puss is you might be allowed to have a cat of your own.'

Serena had sat down on the grass again, and Puss came to sit beside her.

'May I stroke her?'

'Of course, she loves to be cuddled and loved.'

'Mother actually said that she could be in the house?'

'Yes, but I think we won't allow her in the drawing room or dining room. Just the sitting room we are to use and my bedroom.'

'And my bedroom...?'

'Once she has got to know you, yes, I don't see why not.'

Heather said slowly, 'I dare say you're quite nice...'

'I hope so! Now, shall we go and have tea? And perhaps you'll tell me how you spend your days.' Serena picked up Puss and started towards the house, and after a moment Heather followed her.

She said airily, 'Oh, I have to go to school, of course, and you wouldn't be interested in what I do when I'm free—I've friends...tennis and swimming...and I've a bike.'

'Well, yes, of course you have friends...'

'You wouldn't want to do any of the things we do,' said Heather rudely.

'Oh, I don't know. I play tennis and I swim, and

I've ridden a bike for years and years. I drive a car, too.' She smiled at the girl. 'Though I haven't got one of my own.'

'There's a Mini in the garage; Bob and Maisie use it. Perhaps you could borrow it. Not that I'd want to come with you.'

'No, no, of course not—you'd be bored stiff,' Serena said pleasantly.

She was just as pleasant during tea, ignoring Heather's deliberate bad manners, suggesting that she might like to give Puss a saucer of milk. 'Homework?' she asked presently, and was told that homework was something to be ignored as much as possible.

'Oh, a pity. I was going to suggest that when you had done it you might like to give Puss her supper and take her for a little walk in the garden—she likes someone with her.'

Heather eyed her. 'When Timothy is away at school and Mother and Father are away, Mother hires someone to come and stay here—I've hated them all, but probably you won't be too ghastly.'

Serena agreed placidly. Heather was an ill-behaved girl, but probably it wasn't her fault. It seemed to Serena that she was lonely, and only aggressive because she felt that no one loved her. Serena thought that there might be stormy days ahead, but they would be no worse than the years of living with her father and the week or two with Henry.

Mrs Webster telephoned quite late that evening, after Heather had gone to bed. She had rung, she told Serena, to make sure that she had arrived safely, and rang off without asking after Heather.

Serena decided that she didn't like her.

An opinion, if she did but know it, which Mr van Doelen shared with her. He had given Mrs Webster reassuring news of Timothy and was pointing out that there was no need for her to spend the day at the hospital. 'I am sure you will want to go home and see how things are there. You can phone to the hospital each day if you wish…'

'Certainly not, Mr van Doelen. I intend to stay in London, close to Timothy, until he is fit enough to be taken home. There's nothing for me to worry about at Penn. That girl you recommended is there to keep an eye on Heather. She seems to be capable, and reasonably well educated. Of course, one never knows with these young women, but I had to take a chance. Timothy is more important than anything else at the moment. As long as she doesn't go off with the silver!'

She laughed at her joke, but Mr van Doelen didn't so much as smile.

He said coldly, 'Miss Lightfoot is hardly likely to

do that, Mrs Webster, but of course you have only met her briefly, I believe.'

'You know her well?'

Mr van Doelen said coolly, 'I know her family and her friends, as well as Miss Lightfoot. I would not have recommended her to you if I had any doubts about her, Mrs Webster. You will not find anyone more suitable.'

Mrs Webster didn't say any more. Mr van Doelen looked just as usual, with his calm, rather austere good looks, but somehow she sensed that he was angry.

He was indeed angry. He had wanted to help Serena, but he suspected that he had merely helped her out of the frying pan into the fire!

He had been unable to forget her—something which he had found disturbing. His work filled most of his life, though he supposed that one day he would marry; perhaps a woman from his circle of friends. But he had felt no urgency to do so—until he had looked around and seen Serena coming towards him on Barrow Hill.

He had fallen in and out of love like any normal man, light-hearted affairs which had come and gone and been forgotten, but he had taken one look at Serena and known that he had met his true love at last. He had no doubt in his mind that he would make her his wife, but since, at the moment, there wasn't even the remotest possibility of that, he was content to wait. Opportunities to see her again seemed unlikely, but when she left Mrs Webster's employ he would make sure that he was there...

He bade Mrs Webster goodbye with a still austere politeness, and pressed the buzzer on his desk for his nurse to send in the next patient. He hoped that Serena would find life better now that she was away from her brother. He must find a way to go and see her...

Serena was finding life considerably better; Heather wasn't an easy child, and she objected to everything suggested to her—from the changing of a grubby frock to a clean one, the brushing of her hair, the cleaning of her fingernails, to getting up in the morning, getting to school on time and eating her meals. All the same, she had an Achilles' heel: Puss. She showed an unexpectedly tender regard for the little cat and gradually, after the first week or so, she began to show friendliness towards Serena.

She was cautious about it, though, and Serena did nothing to spoil things. She spent all Heather's free time with her, for she never evinced a wish to ask her friends from school to come to the house. Bit by bit she began to respond to Serena's matter-of-fact manner—a game of tennis, swimming in the pool together, visits to Penn to spend her pocket money.

And Serena was able to give Mrs Webster an honest report when that lady telephoned.

Not that Mrs Webster was particularly interested in Heather. She supposed, she had said in her rather loud, aggressive voice, that the girl was behaving herself, and Serena was to be firm with her. As to Serena herself, Mrs Webster made no enquiries as to her comfort, or if she had settled down, and there was no mention of any free time…

Serena didn't mind. She had enough leisure, for beyond seeing to her own and Heather's rooms, helping to clear the dishes and arranging the flowers she was free for several hours while the child was at school. She spent some of them going into Penn to shop for Maisie and, when Bob was amenable, helping him in the garden. But when Heather was home there was no leisure; there was homework to be dealt with—no easy matter since the child avoided doing it whenever she had the chance—and the long evenings had to be filled with tennis or clock golf, and sometimes just sitting in the garden, talking.

The mornings were the worst, though, for Heather lay in bed until the last minute and then refused breakfast, mislaid her schoolbooks and thought up a dozen reasons why she should not go to school that day. Serena wasn't easily beaten.

When Mrs Webster rang one day Serena listened while she was told every detail of Timothy's progress, and when his mother said, 'You have nothing to report, I dare say,' she uttered the speech she had rehearsed so carefully.

'Heather is behaving splendidly, Mrs Webster. I'm sure that she misses you all, but she never grumbles. Of course, she is lonely without her family, and I wondered if you would allow her to have something to love. She is very fond of my cat, and loves to look after her. Would you allow her to have a cat of her own? She would delight in looking after it and feeding it, and it would give her a sense of responsibility.'

'A cat? I have never allowed her to have a pet...'

'She is old enough to look after it herself.'

'Well, I suppose she can have a cat if she wants one—she's such a difficult child, not like Timothy. But if it becomes a nuisance it will have to go.' Mrs Webster added sharply, 'I shall hold you responsible, Miss Lightfoot.'

That evening Heather was particularly tiresome, dawdling over her tea, declaring that she couldn't do her homework since she had the wrong books with her, and then going into the garden to look for strawberries—something she knew she shouldn't do until Bob said that they were ready.

Serena, fetching her indoors for her supper, forebore from scolding her, but as they ate their supper she said, 'I talked to your mother on the phone this morning. It's a pity you're so cross because I had some news for you.'

Heather said rudely, 'All about Timothy, I suppose—spoilt brat. You can keep your news to yourself.'

'Well, I could, but I won't. I asked your mother if you might have a cat of your own, and she said that you could…'

'A cat! I can have a cat? I don't believe you…'

Serena said calmly, 'I thought we might go on Saturday to the Cat Shelter in Penn and you could choose one.'

'You mean that?' Heather got up and flew round the table and flung her arms around Serena. 'My own cat? And he can live in the house with me?!'

'Well, I told your mother that you would train him so well that by the time she came home she would hardly know that he was in the house.'

'You did? You'll help me? Timothy won't be coming home yet, will he? Did mother say?'

'No, but I was told six weeks when I came here, so there is still plenty of time.'

They went to choose a cat on Saturday, and came back with a small thin tabby found abandoned on a bypass. About a year old, they thought, and timid. Heather put her into the cat basket Serena had bought and carried her home. 'I shall call her Tabitha,' she told Serena.

And, to Serena's great surprise, Heather kissed her awkwardly on a cheek.

It was astonishing what Tabitha's arrival to join the household did—Heather changed from a rebellious and ill-mannered child almost overnight. True, she still had bouts of sulky disobedience and sudden flashes of bad temper, but even they grew less. She had discovered that there was something she could love and who would love her in return. And Tabitha did just that. She was a gentle little creature, quickly learning what she might and might not do, accompanying Heather to bed and waiting for her when she got back from school; moreover, she was on excellent terms with Puss.

Watching Heather play with the little creature in the garden, Serena hoped that Mrs Webster would realise that her daughter needed as much attention and affection as she gave her son.

She would miss Heather, reflected Serena. She had grown fond of the child, despite their initial difficulties. And very soon now she would no longer be needed. Mrs Webster had hinted that Timothy's progress was so good that he would be allowed home soon.

Serena counted her wages and thought about the future. Armed with a reference from Mrs Webster, she had a better chance of getting another job. There were dozens of advertisements in the *Lady* magazine for similar work. But there was the question of where she would go while she found something. It might have to be Henry again, for if she stayed in Penn her money would be swallowed up in no time, however cheaply she lived. She might find more opportunities in London. She worried about it a good deal, which was a pity, since kindly Fate had decided to stick her oar in...

Mr van Doelen, over in London on a brief visit to bring into practice his deep knowledge of broken bones, had spent the morning mending, with delicate fingers, a very small boy's shattered body, the result of falling out of a third-floor window. By some miracle there was no head damage, and his painstaking surgery was likely to be successful. But it had been hard work, and he was tired by the time he was ready to leave the hospital, only to find Mrs Webster, lying in wait for him as he reached the entrance beside her.

'I heard you were over here. I hope you aren't going again without seeing Timothy, Mr van Doelen?'

'My intention is to see him in the morning, Mrs Webster. Shall we say ten o'clock?'

'Very well. Mr Gould, who's been looking after him, thinks he's well enough to go home...'

'Splendid. We'll discuss that tomorrow, shall we? Now if you'll forgive me...'

He went out to his car, reflecting that if Timothy were to go home Serena would leave…

He was back at the hospital early the next morning; the small boy was doing well in Intensive Care. Mr van Doelen stayed there for some time, then made his way to his office in the orthopaedic block. Mrs Webster was already there.

He bade her a civil good morning, suggested that she stayed where she was while he and Mr Gould examined Timothy, and went to see the boy. There was no reason why he shouldn't go home; the boy was in plaster and learning to use crutches. Mr van Doelen gave it as his opinion that he could leave hospital within the next few days.

Mrs Webster said sharply, 'I shall make arrangements immediately. Of course he must have a nurse—I know of a good agency—she can go to Penn with us. There will be no need for the girl who's looking after Heather to stay. She can leave at once. I'll phone her today and she can pack her things…'

Mr van Doelen said smoothly, 'If I might suggest that you allow her to stay until the nurse is installed? Some help may be required getting the boy settled in. If you arrange for Timothy to go home in two days' time, I will still be here. I will drive over and make sure that everything is as it should be.'

Behind his quiet voice there was the ring of authority, and Mrs Webster found herself agreeing.

Serena knew that the six weeks of her job were running out, but she hadn't expected Mrs Webster's phone call. She was to be ready to leave in two days' time, and would she fetch Maisie to the phone so that she might give her instructions?

'You will help the nurse when she comes with us,' said Mrs Webster. 'No doubt she will need another pair of hands to make Timothy comfortable, and then you can go.'

'I'll fetch Maisie,' said Serena, and, that done, went into the garden where the two cats were lying together asleep. It had all been rather sudden; she had counted on a week's notice, during which time she might possibly have gone to London, found cheap lodgings and looked for a job—any job... There was nothing for it now but to ask Henry if she might go back there until she found work. And that wasn't the worst. She had to tell Heather...

The child had grown fond of Serena in a guarded way, and she was certainly happier. Besides, she had one or two friends now, encouraged by Serena to come to tea and see the cats. She broke the news as they had their tea, and Heather burst into a storm of tears.

'It'll be beastly,' she sobbed. 'Can't you stay?'

'Well, no,' said Serena, 'but there's a nurse coming with your brother, and I dare say she'll be very nice and like Tabitha, and you have your friends from school. I'll have a word with her when she gets here, and if you make her your friend, you'll find everything will be all right.'

'Where will you go?'

'Oh, I have a brother. I shall stay with him for a while. But if you like I'll write to you. Will you write to me?'

'Yes, and perhaps you could come and see me and Tabitha?'

'I'd like that. You'll have to take extra care of her; she will miss Puss.'

Serena was packed and ready to leave, and prayed that the nurse would be a nice girl. She heaved a sigh of relief when she saw her, for she was young and jolly with a kind face and a ready laugh. But she was competent too, urging Mrs Webster to go into the drawing room and have coffee while they got Timothy to his room.

'He'll be up and about in no time,' she told Serena. 'My name is Maggie—what's yours? Can I come to your room while I give you a resumé?'

'It's your room now,' said Serena, leading the way, and explaining about Heather and Tabitha. 'She's a nice child, but no one has bothered with her.

If you could stand between her and her mother? She has this little cat now, and she sees more of her friends at school. I've let them come to tea…'

'I'll keep an eye on her. When do you leave?'

'Now.'

But when they went back to Timothy's room it was just in time to see Mrs Webster and Mr van Doelen come in. Maggie became all at once very professional, and Serena slipped away and found Heather in the hall.

'They let me come home; I wanted to say goodbye to you. Where's Tabitha?'

'In the kitchen, and the nurse is awfully nice—her name's Maggie; she will be your friend…'

Mrs Webster and Mr van Doelen came into the hall then, and Mrs Webster said, 'Ready to leave, Miss Lightfoot? Heather, you have come to see Timothy, of course. You may go to his room; Nurse is there.'

'You'll write?' Heather flung her arms round Serena.

'Yes, I promise. Remember what I told you.'

Mrs Webster shook hands with Mr van Doelen and then stared at him as he picked up Serena's case and Puss's basket.

He said coolly, 'Are you ready, Serena?' And then, 'I'm giving Miss Lightfoot a lift. Mr Gould will be in touch if you have any worries, Mrs Webster.'

He took Serena's arm and led her out to the car. He popped her into it, put her case in the boot, Puss on the back seat, and got in beside her.

Serena found her voice. 'This isn't…you're very kind…if you would stop at the station…'

'Hush,' said Mr van Doelen in a soothing voice. 'Where had you intended to go?'

'Well, it was all rather sudden, so I'm going back to Henry while I find another job.' She added urgently, 'There's the station.'

'So it is. Unless you're anxious to go back and live with your brother we'll go up to town. I have one or two things to see to, but I'll see you this evening and we'll have a talk.'

Serena said, 'What about? Really, there is nothing for us to talk about. I'm grateful for the lift, but I'll be quite all right if you'd just drop me off at—well, some part of London where I can get a room.'

'I know the very place,' said Mr van Doelen briskly.

CHAPTER FOUR

MR VAN DOELEN had spoken in very decisive tones. Serena, still gathering her wits together, gave up asking questions for the moment. Possibly Mr van Doelen knew of some respectable person who let lodgings, and there was no denying the fact that she might have a much better chance of finding work with London on her doorstep than if she had gone to Henry. She began calculating the cost of bed and breakfast—and would it be quicker if she went to an agency? But that meant paying a fee…

Mr van Doelen glanced at her frowning profile and left her in peace to worry until they were threading their way through the outskirts of London.

'I'm taking you to my old nanny,' he told her. 'She lives in a small house in Chelsea.' He didn't say that he lived there, too. In fact, it was his house; a mews cottage, his pied-a-terre when he was in London.

'Oh, she won't mind? She does bed and breakfast?'

'Oh, yes,' said Mr van Doelen, omitting to mention that he was the one who had the bed and breakfast. He was aware that he was risking Serena's trust, but there had been no time to think of anything else.

He had swept aside the idea of her returning to her brother's house and, although she was a sensible girl, she would have found it difficult to find anywhere to live at a moment's notice. Besides, she obviously had very little money. It was a calculated risk, but one he was prepared to take.

When he stopped the car in a narrow lane behind a terrace of houses, Serena looked carefully around. It wasn't at all the kind of street she had expected. He opened her door and invited her to get out, and she stood for a moment, not speaking; the houses were small, but elegant, with bay trees at their doors and pristine paintwork.

'Come along,' said Mr van Doelen in a no nonsense voice, 'and meet Nanny.'

He unlocked the door of the nearby cottage and urged her into its tiny hall.

'Oh, is this a mews cottage?' asked Serena doubtfully. It was certainly small enough, but it had all the elegance of a smart townhouse.

Before Mr van Doelen could answer her a door opened and an elderly woman came to meet them. She was tall and thin, with a very straight back, a sharp nose in a narrow face and dark eyes. Her hair was almost white, worn in an old-fashioned bun, and when she smiled her whole face lit up.

'Nanny,' said Mr van Doelen, 'I've brought a

young lady to stay for a day or two. Serena Lightfoot. Serena, this is Miss Glover.'

Serena offered a hand, aware that she was being inspected, and waited for someone to say something. This didn't look like a bed and breakfast place; it was far too elegant. She turned an enquiring look on Mr van Doelen, who ignored it, merely inviting her to take off her jacket. 'And I'm sure you'll be glad of a cup of coffee. I'll fetch your case and Puss.'

Serena looked at Miss Glover; she appeared quite unsurprised by his remark. Serena said, 'I don't understand...'

'No, no, of course you don't. Now go with Nanny like a good girl—we will talk presently.'

He went back to the car and Serena followed Miss Glover into the living room, which was low-ceilinged, with windows at both ends and a fireplace opposite the door. It was furnished cosily, with easy chairs and a vast sofa, a scattering of small tables, a drum table under one window and a bow-fronted cabinet holding porcelain and silver against a wall.

'Just you sit down,' said Nanny, in a surprisingly gentle voice. 'A nice cup of coffee's just what you need, and a biscuit or two. Ivo will be back in a minute—you'll be needing to talk, no doubt.'

'Indeed we need to talk,' said Serena crisply. 'I trust he will explain.'

Nanny said gently, 'You may depend on that. A man to listen to is Mr Ivo.'

He came into the room a moment later with Puss in her basket. And Puss, that most placid of little animals, went at once and climbed into Serena's lap.

'You must explain,' said Serena.

'It's quite simple.' He had gone to sit in a chair opposite her. 'Mrs Webster told me that you were to leave as soon as Timothy went home, and as I had arranged to see him to his arrival there it seemed sense to offer you a lift. You didn't wish to go to your brother, and you had had no time to make any arrangements, had you? This seems to be the solution. You can't go traipsing around London looking for a room or a job at a moment's notice. Nanny will be glad of your company for a few days while you find your feet.'

'Is this house yours?'

'Yes. I need somewhere to live when I'm in England, and Nanny needs a home. It suits us both. But if you don't wish to stay here I'll drive you to wherever you want to go. Friends, perhaps?'

'I haven't any friends in London. I'll be glad to stay just for the night, if Miss Glover won't mind. I'm sure I can find somewhere and start looking for a job tomorrow.'

He agreed so casually that she felt, for no reason at all, vaguely put out.

Nanny came with the coffee then, observing comfortably that it would be a pleasure to have someone to stay for a while, and presently Mr van Doelen got up to go. He kissed Nanny's elderly cheek, remarking that he would see her shortly, a wish which he didn't repeat to Serena, merely hoping that she would find a job to her liking without too much trouble and offering her hospitality for as long as necessary.

The house seemed empty when he had gone, and Nanny said, 'He works too hard. Here, there and everywhere from one year's end to the other. He'll be back in Leiden operating in the morning, as cool as a cucumber and nothing but a few hours' sleep on the ferry.'

'He's going back to Holland this evening?'

Serena tried to sound casually interested. He might have told her, she thought, but there again there was no reason why he should. He had done her a good turn; he would have done the same for anyone—all the same, she felt hurt. She would leave in the morning, having no wish to be beholden to him. Indeed, she wished strongly that she had never accepted his offer to stay with Nanny. Upon reflection, she conceded that, since she hadn't known of his plans until they were actually at the door, she hadn't had the opportunity to do so. Her thoughts were interrupted by Nanny's voice.

'What kind of work are you looking for, child?'

Serena improvised wildly. 'Oh, I've always wanted to work in a shop—you see, I've lived for years with just my father, in a small village, and met very few people. It would be so nice to be among people.'

'And your little cat?'

'I think she'll settle down quite happily as long as she is with me.'

'Mr Ivo will want you to stay here until you've found somewhere to live. Have you any money, my dear? London is expensive.'

'My father left me some money, and I have saved my wages while I was at Mrs Webster's house. I have more than enough.'

Miss Glover nodded. 'Good. You don't mind me asking? But I believe you're new to London.'

'Well, yes. I don't plan to stay here, but it is probably the best place to find work. I mean, there's more choice, isn't there?'

'Very likely. Now I'm going to take you to your room and then get our lunch. You have no idea how pleasant it is to have company, Serena.'

After lunch Miss Glover allowed Serena to help with the washing up, and then led the way back to the sitting room.

'Have you known Mr Ivo long?' she asked.

Serena shook her head. 'I really don't know him at all.' She went on to explain how they had met, gently egged on by Miss Glover. Presently that lady said, 'I have some photo albums you might like to see…'

Mr van Doelen as a baby in his pram with Nanny, sitting on his first pony, riding his first bike, in school uniform… Serena turned the pages of his faithfully recorded youth and reached for more formal photos of him in his cap and gown, receiving some award or other from some dignitary, and then several photos cut from newspapers, in some of which he was with pretty girls.

Nanny took the book from her. 'I've a book of cuttings from the papers, too. Famous, he is, but he's never been one to blow his own trumpet.'

'You must be proud of him,' said Serena.

'That I am. Now I'm going to make a pot of tea. If you're going job-hunting tomorrow I'd better find that bus timetable for you; you'll need it. But don't go doing too much; you're to stay here until you've found something to your liking. There's plenty of big department stores not too far away; you'd best try your luck with them first.'

Serena, in bed later, tried to sort out her plans. Everything had happened so quickly that she needed a good think. It was a pity that her sensible thoughts should be disrupted by the image of Mr van Doelen, very clear in her mind. She wondered what he would do when he got to Holland. Did he go home to a wife and children? Where was his home? And when would he return to England?

'I should like to see him again,' she told Puss, curled up on her feet, 'and thank him properly.'

She set off with high hopes in the morning, armed with a list of shops which might offer employment and the bus timetable, but as the day progressed she realised that finding work wasn't easy. And until she had a job she couldn't look for a room.

Miss Glover, over the nourishing meal she provided that evening, assured her that she would find something before long. 'And until you do, you are more than welcome to stay here, my dear. Now, tomorrow, why don't you go further afield?' She mentioned several big stores in the less fashionable shopping streets.

So Serena set off again in the morning, once more optimistic. And once more she was to be disappointed. She told herself not to worry; something would turn up; there must be work in such a vast city for the inexperienced. This time, armed with a newspaper's 'jobs vacant' page, she began on the restaurants. It seemed that others had had the same idea. Either the jobs had been filled or she was asked what experience she had had...

She stopped for coffee and a sandwich, then began the long walk back to the businesses of Oxford Street, and it was on her way that her luck changed.

The supermarket was vast, brightly lighted and crowded, and in one of its windows there was a placard. Shelf-fillers were wanted, it seemed; early-morning and evening work, enquire within.

Serena enquired. The manager looked up as she went into his office. 'Shelf-filler? Strong, are you? Willing to work late in the evening as well as early mornings. Any experience?'

Serena said, no, she didn't. 'But I'm strong, and I don't mind working early and late.' She added, 'I've references…'

He glanced through Dr Bowring's letter and Mrs Webster's brief note with raised eyebrows. 'This isn't quite your cup of tea,' he said.

'No, but I need work, any kind of work.'

'OK. Start day after tomorrow. Live close by?'

'No. I shall look for a room.'

'Better try Mrs Keane, number ten Smith Street, round the corner from here. Several of our girls are there. Clean and as cheap as you'll get round here. You'll be paid weekly.'

He mentioned her wages—hardly generous, but she supposed fair enough.

She thanked him and went in search of Mrs Keane.

The house was one in a row of redbrick villas, shabby, but the curtains were clean. Serena rang the bell and was admitted by a harassed woman who said at once, 'I don't buy anything at the door…'

'The manager of the supermarket told me to come here and ask if you had a room to let?'

'Oh, he did, did he? As a matter of fact, I have. Upstairs back bedroom, or there's the basement. A bit dark, but there's a door into the garden.'

'If I might see it?'

Serena was led down the basement steps and through the door below street level. The room was dark, and smelled vaguely damp, but there was a door into the neglected garden at the back of the house. There was a small out-of-date gas fire, two gas rings on a shelf in a corner, and a sink beside it. The furniture was sparse—a divan bed against one wall, a couple of elderly chairs, a table under the window and a curtained-off corner, presumably for clothes. It was hardly ideal, but the rent, when she asked, was affordable and it would do until she found something better.

'You can use the bathroom on the first floor,' said Mrs Keane. 'Twenty-five pence and don't stay longer than twenty minutes.' She eyed Serena. 'On your own, are you?'

'Yes. But I have a cat...'

Mrs Keane shrugged. 'S'all right, so long as it doesn't come into the house.'

Serena paid a week's rent and began her journey back to Mr van Doelen's house. Neither her job nor her room were ideal, but at least she would be independent. She could start looking for a better job and find another place to live...

A truthful girl, she found it hard to bend the truth to Nanny. She had got a job, she told her, in a large store.

'Not serving at one of those tills?' asked Nanny sternly.

'No, no. It has nothing to do with the customers,' said Serena, which was true enough. 'And the manager kindly told me of someone living quite close by who lets rooms. I've a nice room opening onto the garden.'

'Hot water, I hope, and heating, and proper cooking facilities?'

'Oh, yes,' said Serena, 'all that.' That was true, too, for there was hot water if she boiled a kettle, and two gas rings.

'And when are you starting this job?' asked Nanny sharply.

'The day after tomorrow. I thought I'd go tomorrow to Mrs Keane's to settle in and be ready to start work the next morning. Miss Glover, you have been so kind to me and Puss, and I'm very grateful. I hope one day I shall be able to repay you for your kindness.'

Miss Glover said something which sounded like 'pish' or 'tush'. 'I'm sorry you are going, child. I'm

sure Mr Ivo will want to know that you are settled
in a good job with a future. You must write to me.'

Serena said that she would. And she meant it. Only
she wouldn't give her address…!

She was going to miss the comfort of the little
house, unobtrusively filled with understated luxury.
She was going to miss Miss Glover, too, and most
of all she was going to miss the chance of seeing Mr
van Doelen again.

She packed her bag once more and set off in the
taxi Nanny had insisted that Mr van Doelen had said
she was to have, with Puss and her meagre wardrobe
once more packed.

Now, at the last minute, she had fearful doubts;
supposing she was sacked before she had had the
time to save some money? Supposing Mrs Keane
gave her notice and she had nowhere to go? It would
have been so easy to have stayed in the delightful
little house with Nanny.

'You're a faint-hearted fool,' Serena muttered.
'This is a chance to be independent.'

The room looked depressing, but that was because
the windows hadn't been opened for some time, she
told herself. The door into the garden hadn't been
opened for a long time either; there was a key in the
rusty lock, and she turned it and went into the garden
with Puss under one arm.

It was covered in weeds, but she was relieved to

see that there were no broken bottles or empty tins lying around, and the fences were high. At least Puss could roam if she so wished.

There was a cupboard in the room housing a broom and a bucket. The place needed a good clean, Serena decided. Besides, if she had something to do she wouldn't have time to think about anything else... She put Puss back in her basket, locked the door and went shopping.

She came back presently, laden with scouring powder and furniture polish, soap, dishcloths, tea-towels and bath towels, a kettle and a saucepan and cutlery. Even bought from the local household store they had made a hole in her money, and there was still food...

She went out again, this time to the supermarket, and laid out more money prudently on groceries, and then went back to make a pot of tea in her new teapot and eat bread and cheese for her lunch while Puss toyed with a snack.

By the late afternoon Serena had swept and scrubbed and polished so that the room had lost its shabby air, and with her few photos and small ornaments arranged round it, and a cheap vase of flowers on the table, it looked much more like a home. Pleased with her efforts, Serena found her way up the steps and into the house, and thence to the bathroom for her twenty-five pence worth of hot water.

But first she scrubbed the bath, trying not to think of the luxurious bathroom she had used in Mr van Doelen's house.

The first few days of work in the supermarket were a nightmare. Serena had plenty of good sense, but the work was mind-numbing; endless unpacking of tins and packets and jars, setting them in rows on the shelves, trying to remember what went where. And it all had to be done at speed. The mornings weren't so bad, but the evening shift! There were just a few of them in the vast empty place, something she disliked, and she dreaded walking back to her room. She wasn't a nervous girl, but at night the streets took on a sinister gloom, and there were always groups of youths with nothing better to do, roaming around. But beggars can't be choosers, she reminded herself, and her pay packet at the end of the first week was more than welcome.

After another week or two, after she had bought a few cushions, a colourful tablecloth and new curtains, the room took on a more cheerful look. Besides, she had food in the cupboard by the sink now, and Puss didn't have to go short… I have much to be thankful for, Serena told herself.

After the first few weeks, she wrote to Miss Glover. She gave no address, and described her job and her room in glowing terms, not exactly fibbing but embellishing the truth. It was a letter which

should set Nanny's mind at rest, she decided, pop-
ping it into the nearest letterbox. She had the unbid-
den thought that it would set Mr van Doelen's mind
at rest, too, only she was afraid that he hadn't given
her a second thought.

In this she was mistaken. He had returned to London
for a brief visit some weeks after she had left, and
before Nanny had received her letter. He had listened
to Nanny's rather worried account of Serena's de-
parture, and although he had told her not to worry,
that Serena was a young woman quite able to take
care of herself, he was himself worried.

He had to admit that he had thought about her a
good deal. Until he had met her his work had been
the predominant thing in his life. He would marry,
he had told himself, in due course, if and when he
met a woman he could love. But the years had passed
and there had been no sign of her—until Serena. And
now she had disappeared. He had been a fool to think
that she would stay with Nanny, that it would take
her some time to find work...

He went back to Holland to his clinics and operating and patients, and it was another three weeks
before he returned to his little house and Nanny. She
handed the letter to him this time, and he read it
carefully and then studied the postmark.

'Not a very pleasant part of London,' he observed.

'But at least we know roughly where she is.' He frowned down at Serena's polite missive. 'She may have posted it quite near where she is living or working. If I could find out the exact area—the post office should be able to help.'

'I should never have let her go,' said Nanny.

'Don't blame yourself, Nanny. You could not have stopped her, whatever you said; she is a grown woman, and a sensible one. She must have known what she wanted to do.'

'But you'll find her?'

He smiled at her. 'I shall do my best, Nanny. I can spare a few days; I haven't a great deal to do at the hospital this time.'

It took time and patience to discover someone at the post office headquarters who could help him.

That particular area of London wasn't large. He rummaged around in his study and found a street map of London, and carefully ringed the district. The following day, his clinic over, he drove through the city to the busy crowded streets and rows of small shops, so near the elegant shopping centres and quiet streets of town houses and yet so different in lifestyle. He wasn't sure what he was looking for. Probably, he thought ruefully, he would have to visit every shop in order to find Serena. There were few clues in her letter, but she had told Nanny that she was working in a large store.

Mr van Doelen began his patient search along the main shopping street, crowded by late shoppers and people going home after a long day. It took time; enquiries meant waiting while someone went to find someone else who might know, ending up with the manager with a list of employees. Each time he drew a blank. It was after nine o'clock by now. He was tired and hungry, and even the smaller shops were shut. Tomorrow, he promised himself, and turned down a side street so that he could reverse the car.

He would have overlooked the supermarket, since it was off the main street, but it was brightly lighted still. He got out of the car and tried one of the big glass doors. They were locked, so he went round the side of the building, along a narrow alley, at the end of which there were a couple of men loading trolleys from a small van. The door was open, and Mr van Doelen, bidding them a cheerful good evening, went through it.

It was a very large building, with wide aisles between the towering shelves of food. There were people in the aisles, replacing out-of-date groceries with fresh tins and packets, and halfway down the third aisle he saw Serena. She was on her knees, the better to arrange the lowest rung of tinned peas, and she was unaware of his approach, her mind on her work—she still wasn't as quick as the others.

He stood for a moment watching her, knowing that

now that he had found her again he had no intention of losing her.

When he was close to her he said, 'Hello, Serena.'

She turned her head and he saw the instant delight on her face, so rapidly wiped away that he thought he had imagined it.

She got to her feet. 'Mr van Doelen—how ever did you get here? And should you be here? I mean, we are closed.'

'I walked in and no one stopped me. Why did you run away, Serena?'

She flushed. 'I didn't run away. I told you that I would find work…'

'But you didn't say where. Did you forget to put the address on your letter to Nanny?'

'No, I didn't forget,' she said seriously. 'How did you know that I was here?'

'A process of elimination. When do you finish work, Serena?'

She glanced at her watch. 'In half an hour.'

He nodded. 'I'll be back…'

Serena, loading apricots onto a top shelf, tried to keep her mind on her work. There were a great many tins, and they had to be in position before the place shut down for the night. She couldn't deny that she was overjoyed to see Mr van Doelen, but she must make it quite clear to him that meeting him again would make no difference to her life.

The last tin was in place just as the lights were lowered and everyone got ready to leave. Serena took off her nylon apron, went to the cloakroom for her jacket and made for the entrance opening onto the alley. To get away before Mr van Doelen came looking for her seemed important to Serena, although he might have changed his mind and already gone home.

He was waiting for her by the door. 'Ah, I was afraid that you might have escaped me,' he said briskly. 'I've seen the manager—a most sympathetic man. Considering the circumstances, you can leave as of now…'

Serena gaped at him. 'I can what? But this is my job. No one said that I was going to be sacked. What have I done? Why didn't someone tell me?'

They were out in the alley now, with everyone streaming past on their way home.

Mr van Doelen took her arm. 'You live nearby? Shall we go there and I'll explain.'

'No,' said Serena. 'We won't go anywhere. I don't know why you're here, Mr van Doelen, but just go away. I'm going home.'

'Yes, a good idea. We can talk there.'

'What about?'

He didn't answer, only took her arm and shoved

her tidily into the car. 'Where do we go?' he said mildly, and she, her wits gathering wool, gave him the address.

He didn't say anything as she led the way down the steps and unlocked her door. He stretched an arm and switched on the light, and when they were inside, he shut the door behind him. When he still didn't speak, she said, 'I'm very comfortable here, and Puss has the garden…'

Puss came to meet them, pausing only a moment to rub herself against Serena's legs before making for Mr van Doelen with every appearance of pleasure. Serena turned to look at him.

'I don't know what you want to say, but if you'd say it and go—I don't want to seem inhospitable, but I go to work at half past seven in the morning.'

'Not any more, Serena.' He pulled out a chair. 'Shall we sit down? I want to talk to you.'

She sat down, and he drew up the other chair and sat down too, looking perfectly at home in the shabby room, stroking Puss, who had climbed without loss of time onto his knee.

'I had the devil of a job finding you,' said Mr van Doelen mildly, and reflected that he was about to embark on a future full of uncertainty. Somehow he would find ways and means to make Serena his wife—indeed, he already had a very good idea how to set about that—but would his love be sufficient for both of them? She was no young girl with a head full of romantic nonsense. He wasn't sure that she even liked him… Perhaps he should adopt a friendly, businesslike approach…

'First of all, will you give me an honest answer? Are you happy here, and does the job satisfy you?'

'It's a start, and I have to start somewhere.'

'You haven't answered my question.'

'Well, it isn't quite what I had hoped for.' She saw that he was still waiting. 'No, I'm not happy, but I shan't stay here for ever, you know. There are other jobs.'

'You are wondering why I have been searching for you. We don't know each other, do we, Serena? And yet I feel that we could be friends, enjoy each other's company. I have for some time now considered taking a wife, someone who feels, as I do, that companionship and genuine liking for each other are of more importance than the romantic aspect. I have fallen in and out of love several times, but never once have I wished to marry. But a wife is necessary for a man in my profession. Someone to deal with the social side of life, entertain my guests, accompany me on necessary trips abroad. Above all, someone who will allow me to get on with my work and not make too many calls upon my time. In fact, a business arrangement.'

He had spoken quietly, his eyes on her face. 'I

believe that we might deal very comfortably together.
I need a wife and you need a future. Will you marry
me, Serena?'

She said slowly, 'Supposing I fell in love with
someone? Suppose you fell in love with another
woman? You may not have met her yet…'

'I am thirty-seven, Serena. I have had ample time
in which to meet a girl I wished to marry—the risk
is slight. And you?'

'Me? Well, I've haven't met many men. You can't
count Gregory, can you? I mean, he wasn't marrying
me for love.' She sighed. 'I'm not sure that I believe
in love.'

'But you do believe in liking, in friendship, in
sharing your life with someone who shares your interests and enjoys your company?'

She said slowly, 'Yes, I do believe in that. And I
do like you. I don't know anything about you, but I
liked you when we first met. Sometimes one meets
someone and one feels at home with them at once—
like old friends…'

'Indeed, and that is how I feel with you, Serena.
Comfortable.'

He smiled at her then, and she smiled back, feeling, for the first time in weeks, secure.

'Will you come back to my house and Nanny
now?' he asked.

'I've just paid the rent—in advance, you know…'

'I'll go to see the landlady while you pack your things.'

He got up and put Puss down gently.

Serena said, 'Am I doing the right thing? Allowing you to arrange everything. I wish I had someone to advise me.'

'Try me,' said Mr van Doelen. 'Start packing, there's a dear girl. I have to return to Holland to-morrow, and we must discuss plans.' At her questioning look, he added, 'Our wedding.'

'I haven't said...' began Serena, but he had already gone.

She started to pack at once, and Puss got into her basket and waited patiently. She had been moved around quite a lot lately, and this basement room had been worse than the house at Yeovil. Her whiskers twitched at the memory of the dainty morsels Nanny had provided in her warm, comfortable kitchen. She hoped that she would be going back there.

Serena, her suitcase open half-filled on the divan, had stopped her packing and gone to stand by the window overlooking the dismal little garden. It must have been the surprise at seeing Mr van Doelen again which had caused her to lose her wits. Of course she wouldn't marry him. Of all the preposterous ideas. She would go to the supermarket in the morning and ask for her job back and explain to Mrs Keane that it had all been a mistake...

Mr van Doelen had come back. He saw the half-packed case and said cheerfully, 'Having second thoughts?'

'Second thoughts?' said Serena peevishly. 'How can I possibly think? I don't know whether I'm coming or going.'

He crossed the room and began to pack the small pile of clothes into the case. 'You're coming with me and we're going to be married.' He added in a soothing voice, 'A business arrangement between friends.'

He folded a dress carefully. 'Is there anything else to go in this case?'

She collected up the few photographs, one or two small figurines she had brought from home and her dressing gown, hanging behind the curtained-off corner of the room. She was suddenly tired; she would go with Mr van Doelen, and after a night's sleep she would be herself again, refuse his proposal in a few well-measured words, and go in search of another job. She put the last odds and ends into her case and got her jacket, closed Puss's basket and then told him gently that she was ready to go.

'But please understand that this is just for tonight.'

'No, no, dear girl. Let us be quite clear about it. I have asked you to marry me, and if you have any sense in your head you will accept me. I promise you I shan't think that you're marrying me for my money. I have offered you a bargain. If you will keep your side of it, I shall keep mine. I really do need a wife, and you are so exactly what I had in mind. Now come along. I don't know about you, but I need my supper.'

He gave her a friendly smile. 'If you take Puss, I'll bring the luggage.'

CHAPTER FIVE

Mr van Doelen didn't utter a word as he drove back to Chelsea. Only as they went into the little house he called cheerfully, 'Here we are, Nanny, and we're all three famished.'

Miss Glover came to meet them. 'Supper in ten minutes, and something tasty for Puss.'

She smiled at Serena and said, 'Your room's ready, love. Just you run up and tidy yourself while Ivo brings in your things.'

Serena, speechless, not knowing what to say, did as she was told. When she went downstairs again, Nanny called from the kitchen.

'I'm here, Serena.'

The kitchen was cosy, immaculate, and if there were any labour-saving devices in it they were successfully hidden behind the rows of copper saucepans, the small Aga, the old-fashioned wood dresser and the Windsor chairs round the table, covered by a white cloth and set for three persons.

Mr van Doelen was there, leaning against the dresser, eating a hunk of bread, and Puss was already before the Aga, her small nose buried in a saucer of food. He put the bread down and poured Serena a drink—a dry sherry.

'Just to whet your appetite,' he told her cheerfully, and came and sat down opposite her. They had *coq au vin* and the talk was cheerful, just as though Serena hadn't left. If the talk was mainly between Mr van Doelen and Nanny they didn't remark about it, including Serena in their conversation and not seeming to notice her brief, shy replies.

The *coq au vin* was followed by Queen of Puddings, and when that had been eaten Mr van Doelen said, 'Off to bed with you, Serena; you're asleep on your feet. I'll be here in the morning.'

She summoned her sleepy wits. 'We must talk... I'm not sure—you took me by surprise.'

He said gravely, 'You will be better able to do that after a good night's sleep, Serena.'

He got up and opened the door for her. She wished them goodnight, and with Puss eagerly anticipating a comfortable bed upon which to sleep she went upstairs, to lie in the bath wondering if she had become crazy and what she was going to do about it. She got into bed presently, and fell asleep at once.

She woke early, her sensible self once again, determined to tell Mr van Doelen that, grateful to him though she was for his kindness, she wished to find another job and lodgings as quickly as possible.

She dressed and went downstairs, treading softly,

for the house was quiet and it was still early. Not too early for Mr van Doelen. He put his head round a door in the hall, wished her good morning and invited her to go in.

'A lovely morning,' he observed blandly. 'Nanny will have heard you and will bring us tea. Such a pleasant habit, this early-morning cup. It isn't the general rule in Holland!'

Serena, intent on explaining just why she intended to leave after breakfast, found herself agreeing very politely as Miss Glover came in with a tray and two mugs of tea, the sugar bowl and a plate of biscuits.

'Good morning, Serena,' she said briskly. 'Breakfast in half an hour or so.'

She swept out again and Mr van Doelen asked, 'Sugar?'

Mr van Doelen sat back in his chair behind his desk, the mug in his hand, very much at ease, and Serena, not at all at ease, sipped her tea and looked around her.

It was a small room, its walls lined with books, the desk a splendid example of a George II partner's desk. It was loaded down with papers, a pile of medical journals, and a computer and a stack of what she supposed were patients' notes half hiding the telephone, but the room didn't lack comfort. The carpeted floor was soft underfoot, there were some charming flower paintings between the bookshelves, and the small window had white muslin curtains. There was a small old-fashioned fireplace too. She imagined that in the winter there would be a brisk fire burning in it...

'You wanted to talk?' said Mr van Doelen in an encouraging voice.

'Yes, well, I did—I mean, I do,' said Serena, wishing she was anywhere but where she was at the moment, but, since that wasn't possible, there was nothing for it but to do as he suggested.

'Last night,' she began, 'you took me by surprise. If I'd stopped to think I would never have let you go off like that and get me the sack and give up my room. And all that nonsense about getting married...!'

'I never talk nonsense,' said Mr van Doelen gravely.

She wasn't looking at him. She said sharply, 'Of course you did. You could marry anyone you wished to; that's the advantage of being a man. Don't tell me that you don't have any number of lady-friends.'

He hid a smile. 'Any number,' he agreed equably, 'but never once has it crossed my mind that I wished to marry any one of them.'

'You were joking...'

'I don't joke either,' he told her.

At a loss for words, Serena said, 'Well, then...' Since she could see that wouldn't end the conversation she added, 'That nonsense about getting married.'

Mr van Doelen settled himself more comfortably in his chair. 'Now, shall we start again? I think I made myself clear yesterday evening. If you remember, I told you that I need a wife and you need a future. We get on well together, and that is essential in marriage, do you not agree? Neither of us are in our first youth…'

'I'm twenty-six,' said Serena with a snap.

'Yes, yes. Still quite young, but you have reached years of discretion, have you not? Unlike Gregory, I do not profess my love for you, and there are many such as he around. You are, if you will forgive me for saying so, rather a green girl. I, on the other hand, like you, I enjoy your company, I am sure that we would have a pleasant and undemanding life together and I would do everything in my power to give you a happy life. So if I ask you to marry me once again, Serena, will you say yes? I promise you you won't regret it.'

'You don't think that I would marry just to have a home and no worries?'

'No, I don't think that.'

He looked untroubled and gave her a friendly, reassuring smile.

Serena said slowly, 'It's a bit unusual, isn't it? But

if you're sure you only want that kind of a wife, then, yes, I'll marry you.'

He got up and came round the desk to her chair and took her hand, and for a moment she thought he was going to kiss her. She was disappointed when he didn't.

'We will shake hands on that,' he said cheerfully. 'Shall we have breakfast and discuss our plans?'

'I haven't any plans,' said Serena rather bleakly, and looked for a moment so forlorn that he bent to kiss her cheek.

'We'll see about that,' he told her briskly.

'You would like to marry here?' he asked her over their bacon and eggs. 'You wish your brother to marry us?'

'Matthew? No, I don't think so. He's fond of me, but I don't think he would understand. If it had been Gregory... You see, Gregory expected to marry me; Matthew and Henry both knew him.' She frowned. 'It's difficult to explain...'

'Then don't. I think I understand. Shall we have a very quiet wedding here and return to Holland immediately afterwards?'

She nodded. 'That would be best. There's no one who would be interested, although I dare say your family would want to know?' She buttered some toast and added marmalade. 'I don't know where you live.'

'In a small village near the Hague. I have two married sisters, my father died last year, and my mother lives in Friesland.'

He passed his cup for more coffee. 'I shall tell them when I get back home tomorrow. Our engagement will be announced in the *Haagsche Post* and either *The Times* or the *Telegraph* here.'

She looked surprised. 'Oh, will anyone want to know here?'

He smiled a little. 'I have friends and colleagues here as well as in Holland. I expect you would like to tell your brothers. Invite them if you would like to. I think we might have the Bowrings up for the wedding, don't you?'

'Yes, I'd like that.'

'If you like the idea, a friend of mind could marry us. I'll see about a special licence and we could marry at St Faith's; it's a charming little church in the next street.'

Serena agreed, reflecting how pleasant it was to have someone arranging everything with such ease while at the same time making sure that she was agreeable to what was suggested. After years of her father's bullying and Henry's dictatorial ways it was bliss.

'Not a big wedding,' she said. 'I mean, just ordinary clothes…'

He hid a smile. 'Of course. We shall go over to

Holland the same evening, so there won't be much
time to dress up. I'm sure you'll look pretty in whatever you choose to wear.' Then he asked, 'Have you
enough money to get something suitable for the occasion?'

'Yes, I've Father's five hundred pounds…'

'Then spend every penny of it.'

He watched her face. It held the same enraptured
expression as a small girl offered the fairy on top of
the Christmas tree. He had seen that look before; he
had two sisters.

'I've got my wages from Mrs Webster, too…'

'Spend those as well.'

'It's quite a lot of money.'

'I am well able to provide for you, Serena.' He
said that in a quiet voice which stopped her saying
anything further about the matter.

When they had finished breakfast he said, 'I'll be
half an hour or so phoning. Then will you come with
me and we will choose a ring?' He paused as he went
through the door. 'Would you be willing to marry
me when I next return to London? I've several ap-
pointments here; when I've dealt with them I shall
need to go back home for a time.' When she nodded,
he added, 'And do phone your brothers if you would
like to.' He smiled. 'If I'm hustling you, say so, Serena, but there isn't any reason for us to wait, is
there?'

'No, no, of course not. I'll phone Henry and Matthew and be ready for you in half an hour.'

She phoned Matthew first. He had never bothered much with her, but at least he had never bullied her. He was surprised, but she had expected that. Still he wished her well in a cautious way and called Norah to the phone.

'Quick work,' said Norah. 'I always knew you were a deep one. Getting married so soon, too.' Her voice held a wealth of malice. 'Well, don't expect us to come to the wedding…'

'We hadn't intended inviting you,' said Serena.

Henry made no bones about his disapproval. 'The very idea!' he told her. 'Going off like that and marrying the first man you meet. A foreigner, too. Well, don't expect any help from me if things go wrong.'

'Well, I've never expected help from you, Henry, and nothing is going to go wrong. I'm going to live in Holland for most of the time—that should be a great relief to you!'

'I'm your elder brother,' said Henry at his most pompous. 'I consider myself responsible for your well-being.'

'Rubbish,' said Serena cheerfully. 'Aren't you forgetting that I shall have a husband to look after me?

'Of all the nonsense,' said Serena, putting down the receiver and turning round to see Mr van Doelen smiling in the doorway.

'And that I can promise I shall do, Serena—look after you. Were your brothers disapproving?'

'Yes, but then they have never really approved of me, if you see what I mean, so it really doesn't matter.'

'I've dealt with the special licence and my friend will be delighted to marry us. Now get a jacket and we'll go shopping.'

He took her to a famous jeweller's and they sat in a discreet alcove while they looked at rings together. 'I really don't know,' said Serena. 'I'm not a jewellery person, am I?'

'No, but I think that sapphires would suit you.'

'You choose,' said Serena, rather overcome by the display set before them by the discreet salesman.

It was a choice she would have made herself; she had been held back by doubts as to the price—a splendid stone set in rose diamonds—but apparently Mr van Doelen wasn't bothered about that. He chose it without hesitation, and without asking its cost. Either he was so deeply in love that money didn't matter any more or he was so rich that the price was of no account. Serena was sure that it was the second of these. It fitted; he slipped it onto her finger and the salesman smiled, not only because he had made a good sale but because he was a sentimental man and believed in true love.

Over coffee presently, Mr van Doelen said, 'I'll

get the wedding rings now I know your size. Have you any preference?'

'No, just plain gold.' She admired the sapphire sparkling on her finger. 'This is a very beautiful ring. Thank you, Ivo.'

'I had a word with my bank. If you run out of money, apply to the manager. I'll leave the phone number on my desk. He will want to see you, of course, but there should be no problem.'

'Thank you, but I'm sure I've enough.' She hesitated. 'Shall I need a lot of clothes in Holland? I mean, do you go out a lot? Could I wait and buy things when I get there?'

'A very good idea. We shall go out from time to time. I have friends and family—aunts and uncles and so on—and social occasions to do with the hospitals where I work. But you don't need to worry about that at the moment.'

Serena finished her coffee. As far as she could see she had nothing to worry about at all.

They spent the rest of the day together, the best of friends. It was strange, reflected Serena, that they hardly knew each other and yet they felt so completely at ease together.

When he left that evening she felt bereft. He had bidden her goodbye quite casually, his kiss on her cheek so light and brief that she wasn't sure if she had imagined it. When he had gone she told herself not to get silly and sentimental, and she got out pen and paper and made a list of what she intended to buy. Five hundred pounds seemed a fortune, but from what she had seen in the shop windows it wouldn't go far. She had her wages still; she had meant to keep those against some future emergency, but now she could use at least some of them.

The list grew and she had to start again, crossing out quite a few of the things she would have liked to have bought but which weren't actually necessary. Tomorrow she would go to the shops, not necessarily to buy but just to spy out the land, as it were.

Nanny joined her presently, sitting up very straight in her chair, knitting. She didn't speak for quite a while, but Serena found her presence comforting. Like sitting with your granny, she reflected, someone who didn't talk much, just was there. She added a couple more items to her list, and then crossed them out. She must stick to basics…

'Mr Ivo likes blue,' said Nanny. 'That soft blue like hyacinths. He likes pink too—rose-pink I suppose you would call it. Men like pink…'

'So shall I wear pink or blue for our wedding, Miss Glover?'

'Call me Nanny. Well, it's not for me to say, dear, but blue looks nice, doesn't it? Perhaps you could find a pink dress as well.'

'I thought I'd look for a dress and jacket, something I can wear later on…'

Nanny nodded. 'Very sensible. One of those little jackets. You've a nice shape; you don't need frills and flounces to fill you out.'

The business of buying new clothes suddenly became fun, with Nanny giving snippets of advice. 'You're a sensible girl; you'll know one good outfit is worth more than three cheap ones. Men notice these things.'

Which Serena took to mean that Ivo noticed them. She set off the next morning, Nanny's voice ringing in her ears telling her that she was to stop and have lunch or she would be too tired. 'For you won't find all you want in a day,' she said. 'There'll be a nice tea ready for you when you get back. Go carefully!'

Serena thought how nice it was to have someone who actually minded what she was doing and where she was going. She hadn't felt as happy or as light-hearted for a long time.

By the end of the afternoon she was glad to get back to Nanny and a splendid tea. She hadn't bought anything. 'I saw quite a few things I liked, but I don't want to get anything until I've found an outfit,' she explained.

'Very sensible,' said Nanny, 'and you have time enough. Why not try some of the small dress shops? When Mr Ivo's sisters are over here on a visit they go to a boutique off Regent Street. I don't remember the name off hand, but I'll see if I can find a bill; they always leave the bills with me…'

So Serena set out again in the morning, full of hope. A hope which was to be fulfilled this time. It was nothing short of a miracle that the soft blue dress and jacket in the boutique's window fit her exactly. It was expensive, but she had been prepared for that, and there was still enough money to buy undies and a pretty dressing gown and slippers. She returned triumphant and tried the dress on under Nanny's sharp eye.

'Just right!' said Nanny. 'And such a pretty colour. Now, what else do you mean to buy?'

It took several days to find shoes and a hat for the wedding, as well as a jersey dress, plain and undateable, in a pleasing shade of russet. And then there was just enough over for a skirt and blouses…

Satisfied with her purchases, Serena packed her new wardrobe, hung her bridal outfit in the closet, gave Nanny a hand round the little house and took herself off for long walks in one or other of the parks. Ivo phoned; short, businesslike calls for only a few minutes. Was she well? Her brothers hadn't come to see her? She was happy with Nanny? She replied suitably to these questions and forebore from chatting since he showed no desire to linger once she had replied. He was busy, she told herself, and she thought that he wasn't a man to waste words.

Strangely enough, she had no doubts now. Their marriage was uncomplicated by romance, and she had no longings or fits of jealousy or uncertainties about the future. They would deal comfortably with each other.

Mr van Doelen walked into his house a few evenings later and Serena, winding wool for Nanny, dropped the ball and jumped to her feet.

'Oh, you're back. You didn't phone… Why didn't you?'

'Hello, Serena, Nanny. How very domestic you look.'

Nanny put down her knitting. 'You'll want a meal,' she said placidly. 'About half an hour? You had a good trip?'

'Yes, and I'm famished.'

Serena picked up the wool and sat down again. It seemed that Ivo came and went without fuss; she should have held her tongue. It must have sounded to him that she was critical of him for not phoning. She felt a fool. She must remember for the future.

Mr van Doelen went to his study with his bag and then came back and sat down in a chair from where he could watch her.

'You haven't been bored?' he wanted to know.

'No, no, not at all. I had shopping to do, and I've

explored the parks, and the Reverend Thomas called to see me. He's nice.'

She couldn't think of anything to say then. Oh, for a witty tongue and facile conversation, reflected Serena. She wound the wool as though it was a matter of urgency, not looking at him.

He leaned forward and took it from her. He would have liked to have taken her in his arms and kissed her, but their rather fragile relationship might have been shattered. 'No doubts?' he asked her gently.

'No, of course not. But what about you? You must see how dull I am? That's because I never had any-one to talk to except Father. Won't you find me dull, too?'

'You aren't dull; you're restful. To come home to someone who doesn't start chattering the moment I get there is something I am looking forward to, Se-rena.'

She looked at him then. 'Really? I should have thought that after a day with patients and operating and wards, you would want a little light relief.'

'That, too, but at the right time.'

'Well, I'll remember that,' said Serena as Nanny came back to say that his supper was ready.

'Come and sit with me while I eat?' said Mr van Doelen. 'I want to know how soon you will marry me.'

At the table he told her that he was intending to

be in London for three or four days, no longer. 'We could marry in the late afternoon of my last day and drive to Harwich for the evening ferry. It's a quick crossing by catamaran; we can be home in the late evening.'

'That sounds very sensible,' said Serena, doing her best to sound matter-of-fact. Suddenly the future was crowding in on her. 'The Reverend Thomas won't mind short notice?'

'I've already phoned him. He suggested three o'clock. We can come back here for tea, just us and Nanny and Reverend Thomas and his wife. We'll need to leave soon after.'

'Will you be here before then?'

'I doubt it. I hope to leave the hospital some time after two o'clock, but it may be later. You will wait here with Nanny, will you?'

'Yes.'

It was all rather businesslike, as though he was making an appointment with his dentist. It was disconcerting when Ivo said, 'I am afraid it is all rather rushed, but since we are to have a quiet wedding I believe you understand. I am committed to a good deal of work for the next month or so, and there seems no point in you staying here with Nanny until I'm clear of that!' He smiled a little. 'I promise you you won't be lonely. I have English friends who will be delighted to meet you.'

After supper he told her kindly to go to bed. 'I have some work to do, and I must leave early in the morning, but I should be home in time for us to have tea.'

That was the pattern of the next three days, and on the fourth day they were to marry…

Of course he had already left the house when she went down to breakfast. She had it with Nanny, obediently eating a boiled egg she didn't want and crumbling toast onto her plate. Now that their wedding day had dawned her usual sensible self was engulfed in doubts. Not that she thought for one moment of backing out of it; it was just the last hesitation, like the pause before diving into deep water.

Beside her vague doubts, she knew deep down that their marriage would be a success; they liked each other and enjoyed the same things and neither of them demanded anything from the other. It would be a calm, secure partnership. As if to squash any doubts she might have had, there was a letter from Dr Bowring to tell her that he and his wife would be at the church and how sure they were that she and Ivo would be happy together.

She went for a walk after breakfast, and then, mindful of Nanny's reminder that she had a long journey before her that evening, ate the dainty little lunch the dear soul had prepared. They ate it together in the kitchen and then went, together still, to

Nanny's room so that Serena could help her decide which hat to wear.

And by then, it was time to dress.

The blue outfit looked all right; the new shoes were comfortable and the small-brimmed hat with its satin bow sat elegantly on her light brown hair. She took a last look at herself in the pier glass, caught up the light coat she had had the foresight to buy, and went downstairs to wait for Ivo.

Nanny was in the kitchen, and when Serena poked her nose round the door she was told to go and sit in the drawing room. 'And take care not to get untidy,' said Miss Glover at her most nanny-ish. 'You look very nice.'

Which from Nanny was high praise indeed. Serena hoped that Ivo would agree. Regardless of any damage, she picked up Puss, sitting beside her.

She sat rather primly on a little balloon-backed chair and tried not to look at the clock. If Ivo didn't come soon they would be late for their wedding.

He came a few minutes later; she heard his key in the lock and his quiet footfall in the hall and in a moment he was in the doorway.

'Oh, very nice,' he said, and smiled so that she felt almost pretty. 'I'll be with you in ten minutes or so.'

And he was, in a beautifully tailored grey suit and

a silvery silk tie. He took Puss off her lap and Serena got up as he said cheerfully. 'Shall we go?'

She couldn't think of anything to say as he drove the brief distance to the church and helped her out of the car. It was a small old church at the end of a quiet street. There was no one about; Nanny had gone ahead, and Serena supposed that the Bowrings were already inside. They went inside together and in the porch Ivo handed her a nosegay laid waiting on a bench. Roses and little lilies, green leaves and sprigs of sweet-smelling stocks.

'We are going to be happy together,' he told her, then took her arm and walked with her down the aisle to where the Reverend Thomas was waiting.

The Bowrings were there, and Nanny and Mrs Thomas, turning their heads to smile at them, and there were flowers—a feast of white and pink roses and trailing stephanotis. The afternoon sun shone through the stained glass windows above the altar and the air was fragrant and warm. Serena was aware of all this as she stood beside Ivo; she was aware, too, of feeling happy. Without any doubts as to the future she made her responses in a soft, clear voice and presently they walked back up the aisle, a married couple now, and got into the car and drove back to the little mews cottage where they were joined by the others.

Nanny, still in her wedding hat, served tea: tiny

cucumber sandwiches, miniature scones, fairy cakes and a wedding cake which she had made herself. The talk was cheerful—of the wedding, and promises of a visit to Holland later on and how soon Ivo would be returning to London.

Before long it was time to leave. Puss was tucked into her basket, the cases were put into the car, and farewells said. Serena, in her coat now, her wedding hat sharing the back seat with Puss's basket, got into the car and turned to wave as Ivo drove away, suppressing a sudden small panic that she had burnt her boats and there was no going back.

Ivo said quietly, 'There is still time for you to change your mind, Serena…'

The panic melted before his calm voice. 'No, I don't want to do that. You said that we are going to be happy together and I believe you.'

It took a while to cross London, but presently, with the suburbs thinning to fields and trees, he sent the car forging ahead.

'We'll have a meal on board,' he told her. 'It's a short drive from the Hoek but you may be tired by then, although there will be a light meal for us when we get home.'

'Did you have time for lunch?' she asked.

'No. Coffee and a sandwich. And you?'

'Well, I had time, but I wasn't hungry!'

'We'll make up for that on board. Are you comfortable?'

They found plenty to talk about. Theirs might be a marriage without love, but they were completely at ease with each other; it was as though they had known each other all their lives. Serena heaved a small sigh of content, and Mr van Doelen, glancing at her composed face, allowed himself to indulge in a brief daydream.

The crossing was calm, and they had a meal on board while Ivo patiently answered her questions about his home and his work. A small village, he told her, only a mile or so from Den Haag, and a house his family had lived in for many years. As for his work, he had beds in the principal hospitals in Den Haag, but he lectured at Leiden Medical School and had beds there too, and not only that, he had consultations in other countries as well as being an honorary consultant in London.

'I am a busy man,' he told her, 'but I'm sure you won't be lonely, and when it's possible there's no reason why you shouldn't come with me.'

She assured him that she would like that. 'But you will be sure and let me know if I get things wrong, won't you?'

'Of course. But I don't think that is likely to happen. All my friends speak English…'

'Oh, but I'd like to learn to speak Dutch as quickly as possible. Perhaps I could have lessons?'

'A good idea.' He glanced at his watch. 'We shall be landing very shortly.'

It all looked a bit like England, except for the traffic driving on what she considered to be the wrong side of the road. When he observed that she might enjoy driving herself, she said uncertainly, 'Oh, I don't know—I might forget…'

'Not very likely with everyone else driving as they should. We shall be home very soon now.'

She was a little tired now, as well as hungry, and over and above this she had a sudden feeling of panic. She said rather faintly, 'I'm sure you must be glad to be home,' and heard the uncertainty in her voice.

'Oh, I am, and glad to have you with me.' He dropped a hand on her knee and said, 'Our home, Serena, and I shall do my best to make you happy in it.'

He was driving around the outskirts of Den Haag now and presently turned off into a side-road which in turn opened into a quiet country lane. All at once there were flat green fields and a canal running alongside it. It was dark now, and they had left all signs of the city behind them.

'This is a quiet corner which seems to have been overlooked,' said Ivo. 'It is delightfully peaceful, and so close to Den Haag. I must get you a car as soon as possible.'

'I could bike,' said Serena, and then wondered if a well-known surgeon's wife would be too grand to cycle.

It seemed not, for he said at once, 'Of course you can. Everyone here cycles.'

They had passed a couple of farms standing back from the road, and now there were trees on either side, and in a moment a cluster of small houses round a church.

'The village—we're just round the corner.'

Serena had very little idea what to expect; Ivo had been vague and she had pictured a comfortable villa, substantial and rather dull. But as he turned into a short drive between brick pillars she saw that she was mistaken. The house was brick, faced with stone, with a handsome door reached by double steps, its windows large with elaborate pediments. It wasn't a villa. She studied its handsome façade with faint misgiving. This was a country house, a gentleman's residence of some size.

He had stopped before the front door and she said rather sharply, 'You could have told me...'

He said mildly, 'I hope you won't dislike it. It is home to me. I hope it will be home to you, too.'

He got out of the car and opened her door and helped her out.

'It's a lovely house. I—I was—surprised.'

He took her arm. 'Come indoors and meet everyone.'

CHAPTER SIX

THE person who opened the door was short and stout, white-haired and dignified. Mr van Doelen clapped this dignified person on the back and then shook his head. 'Wim, it's good to see you.'

He had spoken in Dutch; now he turned to Serena. 'Wim looks after the house for me, Serena. He's been in the family for ever. His wife, Elly, is the cook and housekeeper.'

Serena offered a hand and Wim shook it carefully. 'Welcome, *mevrouw*.' He waved an arm and led the way from the vestibule into a broad hallway. There were several people there and he led her from one to the other; Mr van Doelen spoke again in his own language. Whatever it was he said, they smiled and shook hands with Serena in turn. There was Elly, as rotund as Wim, with a round smiling face, a thin, tall woman—Nel, and a short, stout girl—Lien. Also an old man—the gardener, explained Mr van Doelen— Domus, and a leggy youth beside him, Cor.

They all looked pleased to see her, reflected Serena, but she hadn't expected them. She gave Ivo a reproachful look which he ignored.

'Elly will take you to your room,' said Mr van

133

Doelen. 'There will be supper in ten minutes or so.' Serena was led away to where a staircase curved its way up at the end of the hall. It led to a gallery with several doors, one of which Elly opened with a flourish. The room beyond was large, with a four-poster bed facing the two windows. There was a mahogany table between the windows with a silver gilt mirror, flanked by slender silver candlesticks, the bedside tables were mahogany too, each with its porcelain lamp, and there was a chaise longue upholstered in a pleasingly vague patterned brocade; the same brocade draped the windows and formed the bedspread. A very grand room, Serena thought, but a delight in which to sleep. She took a quick look at the adjoining bathroom and opened a door at its other end: another bedroom, rather austere but very comfortable. Well, really, thought Serena, going back to peer at herself in the mirror and poke at her hair, Ivo might have told her that he was so grand.

She went back downstairs and found him in the hall.

'In here,' he said, and opened a door and ushered her into a panelled room with long windows over-looking the garden at the back of the house. He said, 'Before we have supper will you come and meet Casper and Trotter?'

She went with him to the window he had opened and two dogs came racing in: a golden Labrador and a small greyhound. They circled Mr van Doelen, beaming up at him, and he said, 'Here is Serena. Come and say hello.'

Serena bent down to fondle them. 'Oh, they're lovely. Which is which?' And when he told her she asked, 'Why did you call her Trotter? I mean a greyhound…'

'She was discarded as being of no use for racing. The man who threw her out told me that she was only fit to trot! She's elderly, and loves long walks, and Casper loves her dearly.'

It was obvious that Ivo loved her too—and Casper. 'I hope they'll like me,' said Serena. 'I never had a dog; Father didn't like them. Would they go walks with me?'

'Of course. We'll take them tomorrow afternoon and give you some idea of the country round us. I have to go to the hospital in the morning but I should be back for lunch; we can go after that. Now let us have supper—I'm famished.'

'So am I.'

They sat at one end of the long oval table with its gleaming silver and glass. There was a low bowl of flowers at its centre. It looked like a bridal bouquet, but she was too shy to say so. It was Ivo who observed, 'I see that Wim has produced a fitting floral tribute to the occasion. I expect Elly has thought up something equally bridal for us to eat.'

Certainly it was a meal to grace the occasion. Globe artichokes with a truffle dressing, grilled salmon with potato straws, and to crown these baked Alaska. And, of course, champagne.

Serena was hungry, and she did full justice to Elly's cooking. It was late now, but the food and drink had given her a new lease of life. To sit over their coffee talking seemed a splendid idea—only one Ivo didn't share. He said kindly, 'You must be tired; do go to bed. Have you everything you want?'

Serena said politely, 'Yes, thank you. At what time is breakfast?'

'Oh, eight o'clock, but I shall be gone before then. Ask Wim for anything you want. I'll see you at lunch.'

Serena got up from the table and he went to open the door for her. And as she passed him he put a hand on her shoulder.

'Sleep well, my dear. Tomorrow we shall have time to talk. I'll take you round the house and answer all your questions.' He bent and kissed her, a light kiss but at least a kiss… 'You were a beautiful bride,' he told her.

No one had ever called her beautiful before. She said soberly, 'And I'll be a good wife, Ivo.'

She slept soundly in her lovely room, to be awakened by Lien with early-morning tea. When she had showered and dressed and gone down the stairs there was Wim, waiting to escort her to a small room behind the drawing room where her breakfast was laid at a small table by a window. Casper and Trotter were there too, to take up their places each side of her chair, looking expectant. She wasn't sure if they were allowed to be fed at the table, but since there was no one to see they shared her toast…

When she had finished she wandered into the hall, and Wim appeared silently to tell her in his basic English that she might like to walk in the garden with the dogs or go to the drawing room where he had laid out the English newspapers. There would be coffee at half past ten, he added, and lunch at half past twelve when Mr van Doelen would be back home.

Serena thanked him, feeling rather like a visitor no one quite knew what to do with, and went into the garden. A very large garden, she was to discover, stretching away in all directions and bounded by a high brick wall. She explored it thoroughly, with the dogs trotting to and fro, and she admired what she saw. Velvety lawns, herbaceous borders, a rose garden and flagged paths between lavender hedges. And, separated by another brick wall, a kitchen garden, filled with orderly rows of vegetables. There were fruit trees too, and stooping over a bed of lettuce was old Domus. He straightened up when he saw her and she wished him good morning, wishing she could talk to him. She must learn to speak Dutch as quickly as possible…

She went back into the house presently, and had her coffee and glanced through the papers, but she soon got up, feeling restless, and went into the hall and began opening doors. The drawing room, the dining room, the little room where she had had breakfast. That left two more doors as well as the baize door leading to the kitchen quarters. Ivo's study. She didn't go in, only stood at the door looking at the great desk and the chair behind it, the shelves of books, the powerful reading lamp. This was where he would come to work, she supposed, undeterred by the household's activities. She closed the door and crossed the hall to the last door. The library. Its windows overlooked the side of the house and the walls were lined with books.

She walked slowly, looking at titles, Dutch, German, French and, thankfully, plenty of English. And not only medical tomes, but a fine assortment of the English classics and a dozen or more modern bestsellers. There were magazines on one of the library tables, and comfortable chairs in which to sit and read them. Of one thing she was certain: she would never be bored; a lovely old house, a magnificent garden, the dogs and the friendly people who lived there… And Puss, of course, already placidly at home.

She perched on the library steps, studying the spines of the books above her, and was there when Ivo came in.

She put the weighty volume she was holding back in its place and got off the steps. She said a little breathlessly, 'You don't mind? It's such a beautiful library.'

He crossed the room. 'Of course I don't mind; it is your library too. You like books and reading?'

'Yes, but I've never had much spare time. Have you had a busy morning?'

'Yes, and I shall be busy for a week or two. But I intend to find the time to take you round the hospital; everyone is anxious to meet you.'

'Oh—you mean the medical staff and the nurses?'

'Yes, and their wives and husbands. But it will be just the medical staff to start with. In three or four days' time, if you would like that.' He added, 'Perhaps you would like to go shopping? You could go in with me tomorrow morning and you can have the day to yourself.'

She thought of the few pounds she had in her purse. He was suggesting in the nicest possible way that she needed the kind of clothes his wife would be expected to wear.

He watched her telltale face, and added in a matter-of-fact way, 'I've an account at several of the bigger shops, and I'll let you have an advance on your allowance.'

He strolled across the room towards the door. 'Shall we have lunch? Then we'll go for a walk with the dogs. Time enough to show you round the house after tea.'

Serena hadn't moved. 'I haven't any money of my own, you know that, but I don't like taking your money, Ivo.'

He leaned against the door he was holding open. He said in a level voice, 'You are my wife, Serena. You will share everything I possess; you will buy all the clothes you want and anything else you fancy.' He smiled then. 'I'm proud to have you as my wife and I want you to know that. And let us have no more nonsense about money. Buy what you like and send me the bills.'

'Oh, well,' said Serena, 'put like that it seems very sensible. Thank you, Ivo.'

They lunched together, talking about this and that in the comfortable manner of old friends, and presently took Casper and Trotter for a walk. They went through the village and Serena tried not to mind being stared at. She was, she supposed, a bit of an event in the quiet little place. They stopped to speak to several people, who beamed at her and shook hands and laughed a great deal with Ivo. But once clear of the village he took her down a narrow lane with flat meadows on either side. There were the black and white cows she'd expected to see, and farms, widely spaced, with their great barns and a few sheltering trees.

'Is all Holland like this?' she wanted to know.

'No, by no means. Limburg, in the south, is quite hilly, and in the north there is more space. Lakes too. I go there in the summer and sail. I've a small farm in Friesland—a few sheep and cows, hens and ducks and geese. Will you like that?'

'Oh, yes, but I like your house here. It's old, isn't it? It feels like home...'

He took her arm. 'It is home, Serena. Our home.'

He whistled to the dogs and they turned back, going through the village again where they were stopped by even more people.

Serena, shaking hands and smiling and murmuring, hoped that they approved of her.

They drove into Den Haag early the next day, and Ivo parked the car and walked her round the shopping streets, pointing out where she could have coffee and lunch, showing her how she could get to the hospital if she needed to.

'But you should be all right,' he told her casually, 'I should be ready by four o'clock. Just tell the porter who you are and they'll tell me that you're there.' He gave her a quick look. 'You'll be all right on your own?'

Serena, her purse stuffed with notes, assured him that she would.

The arcade opposite the big departmental store looked promising. She went along its length, looking in all the windows—boutiques, jewellers, smart cafés, magnificent china and glass. She retraced her steps and paused at a boutique halfway down the arcade. There was a dress in the window, its accompanying jacket thrown carelessly over a little gilt chair. Honey-coloured, a silk and wool mixture. Very plain and simply cut— 'And very expensive,' muttered Serena, opening the door.

It was a perfect fit. She paid its outrageous price from the roll of notes in her purse and went off in search of shoes. Which naturally led to the obligatory purchase of tights. She stopped for coffee then, before going into De Bijnkorf in search of undies and something to wear at home. Prudently making sure that Ivo's account could be used by her, she went from one department to the other: simple dresses, skirts, tops, blouses, cardigans. She stopped for lunch then, since there was a restaurant there, and then went out into the street again. She had acquired a splendid wardrobe, although it was by no means complete. She needed a raincoat, and what about something for the evening? Ivo had said that he had friends. Presumably they would be asked out to dinner.

She began another round of the shops, not sure what she was looking for.

It stared her in the face from a shop window in another arcade. Pale pink silk and chiffon, simple, relying on the cut and the delicate colour. Its modest neckline and long tight sleeves were just right for dinner out or an evening with any of Ivo's friends. She bought it, and went in search of high-heeled strappy sandals…

And, after that, 'Enough's enough,' said Serena, and went to one of the smart cafés for a cup of tea. She would take a taxi to the hospital, she decided. She was drinking her second cup when Ivo sat down opposite to her at the little table.

'I finished early,' he told her, 'and decided to come and give you a hand with your parcels.' He glanced at the pile on the floor. 'You have had a successful day?'

'Oh, very, thank you. Would you like tea?'

'It's coming. Are you going to have one of these cakes?'

'I've already had one…'

'Then have another while I drink my tea. You found shopping easy? No language problems?'

'No, none at all.' She selected a mouthwatering confection of chocolate and whipped cream. 'Have you had a busy day?'

'Yes.'

She waited for him to say more, and when he didn't she said, 'I'm not just inquisitive; I'm really interested.'

He gave her a thoughtful look. 'Yes? Then I shall get into the habit of boring you each evening with my day's work.'

'I shall like that.' She finished her cake and they went together to where he had parked the car and drove back home, silent now, but it was the pleasant, companionable silence of old friends or a long-married couple. And that was what Ivo wanted, reflected Serena with a pang of sadness. But she had no reason to feel sad, she told herself, for he seemed content...

For the next few days she saw very little of him, for he spent them in Leiden and Utrecht, operating. He got home in the early evening, looking tired, so that she forebore from questioning him, but sat quietly with the wool and needles she had bought in Den Haag, intent on knitting a sweater for his Christmas present. True, that was some way off, but she was a slow knitter and the pattern was complicated.

She was rewarded one evening.

'You are a very restful woman, Serena. I find myself thinking of you sitting there with your knitting when I'm confronted by an over-large clinic and you act upon me like a tranquilliser. I shall be back here in a couple of days. We will go round the hospital together so that you can meet everyone. You're not bored? I've had to leave you alone…'

'I couldn't possibly be bored. Trotter and Casper take me for long walks, and I go to the kitchen each morning and Elly and I talk—about food and so on, with Wim helping out. I know quite a number of Dutch words already.'

'You shall have lessons. I'll arrange that for you. So, will you come with me on Friday morning?'

'With pleasure. I've been longing to wear the dress I bought.'

He raised his eyebrows. 'Only one? We must remedy that!'

'Oh, I bought some skirts and tops, and another dress or two. I'm wearing one of them.'

'And very nice, too,' said Mr van Doelen quickly; he hadn't noticed the dress, he saw only Serena's face and her large dark eyes. As far as he was concerned she could be wearing a sack. He made a mental note to be more observant in the future.

When she joined him at the breakfast table on Friday morning he got up to pull out her chair and kiss her on her cheek. 'You look delightful,' he told her, and meant it. The simple dress suited her, and the pleasure of wearing it had added a sparkle to her eyes and pink to her cheeks.

'Will it do?' she asked anxiously. 'There's a jacket to go with it…'

'It's just exactly right.' He must buy her a brooch, he thought, and some pearls—and there was that diamond necklace of his mother's...

He took her straight to the consultants' room behind the vast entrance, and just for a moment she panicked as he opened the door. The room appeared full of well-dressed men, all staring at her. But the moment was over. A tall grey-haired man and a small woman with a sweet face were smiling at her...

'The hospital *directeur*,' said Ivo, 'and his wife. Duert and Christina ter Brandt—my wife, Serena.'

'I've been dying to meet you,' said Mevrouw ter Brandt, 'well, we all have—I wanted to come and see you, but Duert said I must wait until you had settled in.'

Duert ter Brandt smiled at her and shook hands. 'We are delighted that Ivo has married at last and we hope you will both be very happy. I'm sure you will soon have many friends.'

And after that she was led from one person to the next, smiling and murmuring politely and forgetting names as fast as she was told them. When the last introduction had been made they went from group to group while they drank coffee and ate little biscuits, and presently Serena found herself without Ivo, smiling at a man younger than the rest, who took her coffee cup from her and, standing in front of her, screened her from the others.

'I'm sorry, I've forgotten your name,' said Serena.

'Dirk—you don't need to know the rest of it. How is it that Ivo found you first? I've been looking for a girl like you all my life…'

He was being familiar, decided Serena, and wasn't sure if she liked that. But it was rather fun to be chatted up—no one had ever done it before… She decided to ignore his remark and asked, 'Are you a doctor or a surgeon?'

'Doctor; I couldn't aspire to the surgical heights of your husband.' And, at her surprised look, 'Only joking—he's brilliant. Are you going to be happy here in Den Haag?'

'Yes, of course. And we don't live in Den Haag; our home is in the country.'

'May I come and see you there?'

'I'm sure we'll both be delighted, but not just yet.'

She glanced round and caught Mevrouw ter Brandt's eye. 'I must speak to Mevrouw ter Brandt.' She gave him a nod and a smile and crossed the room.

'You must come to tea—and call me Christina; I'm years older than you, but we're both married to Dutch medical men so we have a lot in common.' Christina smiled a little. 'What did you think of Dirk Veldt? A great one for the ladies. Come to tea on Monday; get Ivo to bring you. You must meet the children. I've three—a girl and two boys.'

'I'd like that very much, thank you.'

Serena felt an arm on her shoulders and Christina laughed. 'Ivo, I've invited Serena to tea on Monday. Will you bring her? Come early—it is your clinic afternoon, isn't it?'

'Two o'clock not too early? May I collect her around five o'clock?'

They said goodbye then, and Duert ter Brandt shook hands once again and said kindly, 'You must both come to dinner soon.' He clapped Ivo on the shoulder. 'You're a lucky man, Ivo.'

He kissed Serena, and Christina gave her a hug. 'Are you going round the hospital? We won't keep you, then; it will take the rest of the morning.'

Which it did. But, since Serena was interested in everything she saw, that didn't matter. Ivo took her home to lunch and then went back to work. 'But I'm free tomorrow,' he told her. 'We'll drive up to the farm.'

It was a cool, crisp morning when they left soon after breakfast the next day. He took the road through Alkmaar and across the great *dijk*, and once in Friesland turned away from the main road toward Sneek. There were lakes on all sides, and large farmhouses backed by vast barns, and the roads were mostly brick and narrow. Presently they reached a scattering of houses, too small for a village, and a mile or so further on Ivo turned in through an open gateway and stopped before a farmhouse standing back from the road.

A tall, thick-set man came round the corner of the house, calling a welcome, thumping Ivo on his shoulder and then shaking hands with Serena, and a moment later he was joined by a woman, almost as tall as he. 'Abe and Sien,' said Ivo, 'who run the farm for me.'

They all went indoors then, to drink coffee and eat little sugary biscuits, with Ivo patiently translating the conversation to Serena. It was all about sheep and cows and poultry, and presently she was taken to see the livestock before going back to the kitchen to sit at the table and eat sausage and red cabbage and delicious floury potatoes. And although she couldn't understand a word Abe and Sien were saying, Serena enjoyed every moment of it.

She was shown over the farmhouse next. It was a comfortable dwelling: a large living room, well furnished—although it was obvious that the kitchen was the hub of the house—and upstairs the bedrooms were large and airy.

'We can come up here for a weekend and go sailing if you like,' said Ivo, and Serena could think of nothing nicer. Although she had to admit that she had no idea of how to handle a boat.

'I shall enjoy teaching you,' said Ivo.

A lovely day, thought Serena as they drove home.

They went to church on Sunday, took the dogs for a walk, with Puss tucked under Serena's arm, and spent the evening pottering around the garden. After dinner, in the library, Ivo showed her the books she was most likely to enjoy.

A truly perfect day, and her visit to Christina to look forward to tomorrow. It was as she was going up to bed that Ivo came to the bottom of the staircase to ask, 'What did you think of Dirk Veldt?'

'He seemed a very pleasant man. Very good-looking too. Is he married?'

'No. Don't get too friendly with him, Serena.'

Surprise kept her silent for a moment then she said, 'Well, I'm not likely to see him, am I?'

She was on the point of adding that she was old enough to choose her own friends, but she thought better of it, for Ivo had sounded like a man who expected to be listened to and obeyed. And, after all, they had been married with old-fashioned vows, and one of them had been to love, honour and obey. Well, she honoured him, even if she didn't love him, so she would obey him—up to a point!

She said sweetly, 'Very well, Ivo. Goodnight.'

The ter Brandts lived in a large house in a quiet, tree-lined avenue in Scheveningen. As Serena and Ivo mounted the steps to its imposing front door it was opened by an elderly white-haired man, rather stout.

Ivo shook his hand. 'Serena, this is Corvinus, who looks after Duert and Christina so well.'

A remark which Corvinus received with a dignified inclination of the head before leading them from the vestibule into the hall, just as Christina flung open a door and came to meet them.

'Oh, good, you're here. Ivo, must you go away at once, or can you stay for a while?'

He bent to kiss her cheek. 'Don't tempt me, Christina, I've a clinic in ten minutes or so. May I collect Serena around five o'clock?'

'And stay for a drink. Duert should be home by then.'

He turned to go, dropping a light kiss on Serena's cheek as he went.

A brotherly peck, reflected Christina. I wonder why?

She said cheerfully, 'Come into the sitting room. It's rather untidy but I'm sorting things for a jumble sale and the children's puppy and my cats have made it worse.'

It was a lovely room nevertheless, and splendidly furnished, although the vast sofa was covered by a variety of odds and ends and the big rent table under the window was piled with boxes. There was a puppy asleep in a basket and two cats curled up on one of the chairs.

It was obvious that Christina had been sitting on

the floor, cutting something from a paper pattern.
'Corvinus doesn't approve of me making the room
untidy; I have to clear everything up before Duert
comes home—not that he would mind.' She smiled
as she spoke and added for no reason at all, 'We've
been married for seventeen years.'

Serena got down on the floor with her hostess. It
was delightful to find someone so friendly and un-
self-conscious. She said, 'May I help?'

'Would you? That bag of wools—if you'd sort
them out? Some of them are in a fearful tangle. You
must come to the jumble sale. I've got a stall and I'll
need help. It's on Thursday afternoon.'

'I'd love to, but I don't speak Dutch...'

'That won't matter as long as you can handle the
money. You'll be the star attraction; we were so delighted when we saw your engagement in the *Haagsche Post*. Ivo's far too nice not to be married, and
I'm so glad it's you.'

Christina rummaged in her workbasket. 'Now, tell
me all about yourself.'

'Well, I'm not a bit exciting, I'm afraid. I lived at
home looking after my father until he died—that's
when I met Ivo. At least, we met out walking and
talked a bit, although I didn't know who he was...'

Christina made a small encouraging sound and Serena found herself telling her about her brothers and
her difficult father. She had to talk about Ivo too, of

course, but she glossed over her stay in London, merely saying that they had decided to marry quietly since Ivo had had to return to Holland.

'Very sensible,' said her hostess comfortably. 'I'm sure you will be happy here. You'll be swamped with invitations to dine and have coffee with all the wives, but they're all nice women; you'll like them. Gossipy, of course, but you can take that with a pinch of salt. They've been marrying Ivo off for some years…'

And then Corvinus came in, tut-tutting at the state of the room. Tea, he told his mistress, would be served in the garden room, if the ladies cared to go there very shortly.

Christina said something to him in Dutch to make him smile and added, 'We may have ten minutes to finish what we are doing.' When he had gone she said, 'He's been with Duert for years. When I first came here to work at the hospital it was he who met me at Schipol, and he's been my friend ever since.'

Serena finished sorting the wools, put them tidily in a box, and went with her new friend out of the room and across the hall to a much smaller room, very cosy, its window overlooking the garden. And here they had their tea.

'English afternoon tea,' said Christina with a twinkle, 'and in the winter Duert has crumpets sent from

Fortnum and Mason.' She added simply, 'He spoils me...'

Serena felt a sudden pang of envy—to be so loved... The thought was followed immediately by the heartening one that Ivo might not love her but his liking had been deep enough to make him want her for his wife.

They lingered over tea, and they were still there when the two men came in together. Duert bent to kiss his wife and smiled at Serena. 'You found enough to talk about?' he asked.

Ivo had come to stand beside her chair, stooping to kiss her cheek.

'Indeed we did,' said his wife. 'Serena must come again and meet the children. She's going to help me at the jumble sale...'

'A nerve-shattering event for all but the most strong-minded women!' They all laughed as Duert said it.

They went soon after that; Ivo had to return to the hospital to check a patient's condition.

'But you'll come to dinner soon,' said Christina. 'We'll have a few people in to meet you. Serena must get to know everyone as quickly as possible.'

'You enjoyed your afternoon?' asked Ivo as they drove back to the hospital.

'Very much. I didn't know that Christina had been a nurse here.'

'Yes, but she and Duert met in London. I dare say she will tell you about it.' He didn't say more, and there was no chance to ask him since they had arrived at the hospital.

Ivo parked the car near the entrance, assured her that he would be a mere five minutes or so, and went into the hospital. The main door was glass, and she could see him walk the length of the entrance hall and then start up the staircase at its end.

It was comfortable and warm in the car, and she was content to stay there and mull over her pleasant afternoon, but she rounded herself presently and glanced at her watch. The five minutes was already fifteen...

She looked through the doors and watched several people passing to and fro, but there was no sign of Ivo. Several more minutes had passed before she saw him, walking slowly from the staircase. There was a woman with him—too far off to see her clearly—but she looked young, talking animatedly, and Ivo, his head bent, was listening. They slowed their walk and stood near the door so that Serena had a better view. The woman *was* young and pretty, and well dressed, and she had a hand on Ivo's arm.

Serena was surprised at the sudden rage which shook her, made worse when Ivo put a hand on the woman's shoulder. They had all the appearance of old, familiar friends, laughing together. Serena had the urge to jump from the car and remind Ivo that she was his wife. Then common sense took over. Ivo had friends whom he had probably known long before he'd met her, and she had no business to mind about that. It would be different if she loved him...

She looked away from the door. That was the trouble, of course. She did love him! She had never fallen in love before—you couldn't count Gregory—and she had had no idea. She drew a long, calming breath and took another look at the door. They were saying goodbye—no formal handshake—and Ivo was walking out towards the car.

CHAPTER SEVEN

Ivo got into the car beside her.

'Sorry I was longer than I expected.' He gave her a brief, smiling glance and she waited for him to tell her about the girl. Only he didn't. Serena swallowed back the words she longed to utter; this was something she must sort out for herself, a complication she hadn't even thought of. And if she had discovered that she had fallen in love with Ivo before they had married, would she still have married him? Common sense said no, but her heart said yes. This was something she would have to learn to live with. She would have to fill her life with other interests, leaving Ivo free while at the same time fulfilling her wifely duties. And she might as well start straight away...

'Your patient was all right?' she asked. And when he nodded added, 'You don't mind if I help at the jumble sale? Christina thinks it would be a good way of meeting a few of her friends.'

'I agree. Get to know as many people as you can, my dear, then when I'm away you won't be lonely.' He sounded casual. 'I'm going to Madrid—there is a case there I've been asked to operate upon. I won't take you with me for I shall be too busy.'

She kept her voice pleasantly interested. 'When do you go?'

'On Thursday.'

They were home by now, and the rest of the evening was spent pleasantly enough, walking the dogs and having a leisurely dinner. But as they left the table Ivo said, 'I've a good deal of work to do. I'd better say goodnight, Serena.'

So she sat for a while with Puss for company and her knitting to keep her fingers occupied. Her head was occupied too, but not with knitting.

Ivo was to take an afternoon flight to Madrid but first, he explained, he would have to go to the hospital. So Serena ate a solitary lunch on Thursday after bidding him a cheerful goodbye.

'I'm not sure when I'll be back,' he'd told her, 'but I'll phone.'

She hadn't been able to resist asking, 'A few days? weeks?'

He'd smiled down at her. 'Days.'

She had nodded and smiled brightly, longing to say that she would miss him.

Wim was to drive her to the ter Brandts' house after lunch, and because she felt unhappy, despite all her good resolutions, she decided to go earlier than was necessary. Wim could set her down in Den Haag and she could get the wool she needed for the sweater and take a tram to Scheveningen. The dogs had had their walk in the morning, so she bade Puss goodbye, got into Wim's little Fiat and was driven into the shopping streets. There was still plenty of time before she needed to be at the ter Brandts' house, and almost without thinking, she turned her steps to the hospital. Ivo would be gone, but just to look at the place would make him seem nearer...

She was idling along, close to the hospital now, when Ivo's car swept past her. And sitting beside him was the girl. She was talking animatedly but Ivo was looking ahead, which was a good thing otherwise he might have seen Serena's astonished face.

She stood stock-still, not quite believing her eyes. A woman with a pushchair and several small children rather pointedly nudged her out of the way and she turned on her heel and walked back the way she had come. She wanted to go home, to go into the garden and sit quietly and think, but there was the jumble sale. She stopped a taxi and got to the ter Brandts' house only a few minutes later.

Christina, coming to meet her as Corvinus admitted her, took one look at her face and said briskly. 'Good, you're on time. I hope you've come prepared for hard work. Did Ivo get away in time to catch his plane?'

She bustled around, carrying on a conversation which needed no replies, for she could see that Serena was in no state to chat. Had she and Ivo quarrelled? she wondered. The girl looked as though she could burst into tears. Christina wisely forbore from asking, but hurried Serena out to her car and drove to the hall where the sale was to be held.

Mercifully there was so much to do when they got there, and she was introduced to so many people that Serena had no time to think, and when the doors were finally closed Christina drove her back and gave her tea before getting into the car once more and taking her back home, all the while chatting quietly about nothing much, relieved to see the colour come back into Serena's cheeks. She didn't stop.

'I must get back home; Duert likes me to be there when he comes back. He mulls over his day with me. I expect Ivo does the same?'

Serena conjured up a small smile. 'Oh, yes, he does.' But she sounded so forlorn that Christina just stopped herself in time from asking what was wrong.

Back home later that evening, with the children in their rooms, she looked across at Duert, sitting in his chair, reading the paper.

'There's something wrong,' she told him. 'Serena isn't happy—in fact she was on the point of tears. Do you suppose they've quarrelled?'

Duert put down his paper. 'My darling, it is perfectly natural for couples to quarrel, and they are neither of them young and foolish.'

He smiled at her and she smiled back, sure of his

love and of her love for him. She said, 'We're happy, aren't we?'

'Blissfully so, dear heart, and so will they be, but give them time.'

Serena ate a solitary dinner, took the dogs and Puss into the garden and went early to bed, explaining to Wim that she had a bad headache.

'More like she's missing the master,' he told Elly. 'Pity she couldn't have gone with him.'

'He wouldn't take her to Madrid—all those foreigners.' She sighed sentimentally. 'Missing him, of course, and he'll be glad to get back home to her.'

Serena didn't sleep much. She did her best to be sensible; she must not let imagination run away with her. Perhaps the girl was one of his assistants, or a special nurse to look after his patient. She had been very well dressed for a nurse, and she hadn't looked like one. Ivo would phone her in the morning and she would ask in a casual manner. No, she couldn't, because he would know that she had seen them together.

Her mind in knots, Serena's imagination became more and more vivid as the night advanced. It was almost daybreak when at length she dozed off.

She took the dogs out directly after breakfast, intent on being in the house if Ivo should ring, but there was no phone call; she pottered in the garden,

never far from the house, but although various of the
ladies whom she had met at the jumble sale phoned,
with invitations to coffee or tea, there was nothing
from Ivo. 'He's been too busy,' she told Puss, and,
since there was nothing better to do, took the dogs
for another walk.

He didn't phone the next morning either, so that
by lunch time she was not only desperately unhappy,
she was in a fine rage. Just because they weren't
madly in love with each other—well, he wasn't anyway, she amended—that didn't mean to say he could
forget her the moment he left home.

She pecked at her lunch and went to the library to
look for a book. It was while she was there that Wim
came to tell her that she had a visitor.

'Dr Veldt, *mevrouw*,' said Wim, 'in the drawing
room.'

Serena put down her book. 'Doesn't he want to
see my husband, Wim? Perhaps he doesn't know that
he's away. I suppose I'd better go.'

Dirk Veldt was standing looking out of the window, but he turned as she went into the room.

'I thought that you might be lonely now that Ivo
is away,' he said, and crossed the room to take her
hand. 'Too bad of him to leave his bride so soon
after the wedding.'

Serena said calmly, 'Good afternoon, Dr Veldt.

I'm not in the least lonely, although it is kind of you to ask.'

'I thought you might like to drive into the country? The real country.' He sneered a little. 'The Veluwe is beautiful at this time of the year.'

'It's a famous beauty spot, isn't it? But, no, thank you.'

She hadn't asked him to sit down, and waited quietly for him to leave. He was an attractive man, and amusing, but she wasn't sure if she liked him.

He smiled. 'Oh, well, there was no harm in asking. Perhaps another time—Ivo goes away quite frequently, you know. Madrid this time, wasn't it? Some VIP, I suppose, with a broken leg. Still, he'll have Rachel to keep him company.' He smiled widely at her.

She met his gaze with an answering smile. 'Yes, it's a good thing that he has,' said Serena, with what she hoped was just the right amount of casual interest. 'I'm sorry that I can't ask you to stay for tea…'

It was just as well that he left then, otherwise she might have burst into tears. He was a mischief-maker, with nothing better to do than stir up trouble, she told herself. All the same, he had sewn the seeds of doubt in her mind.

She must forget his sly remarks, she told herself. If she hadn't fallen in love with Ivo she supposed they wouldn't have mattered, but now it was hard to banish them. She went back into the library, determined to ignore them, but when at last Ivo telephoned that evening she found it hard to talk to him. In reply to his questions as to how she had spent her days she gave stilted answers, and she didn't tell him of Dirk's visit, only enquired as to his work.

'I hope to be home in a couple of days. You aren't lonely?'

'No, no. There's so much to do—the dogs, you know—and—and…' She was stuck. 'Do you want to speak to Wim?'

His voice sounded suddenly cool. 'Yes, please. Goodnight, Serena.'

She went to see Christina in the morning; there was to be coffee, and there would be several wives there whose husbands were colleagues of Ivo. She dressed carefully, anxious to make a good impression, and did her face and hair with a good deal more attention than she usually paid them. She must remember that she was a happy bride…

There were two or three wives of her own age, one or two slightly older women, and an elderly lady with an air of great importance. The *burgermeester's* wife. Serena was being circulated from one group to the next, and soon she found herself sitting on one of the sofas beside her and submitted to the questions put to her.

'You should be happy,' pronounced her companion. 'Ivo is a most successful surgeon, and not only in Holland. A charming man too. He has had many opportunities to marry.' She smiled—a rather mean smile, Serena thought. 'And he ignores some of the most eligible young women in his own country and marries you. Men are so unpredictable.'

Serena wondered if she was being deliberately rude or whether she was just tactless. She said, 'Yes, they are, aren't they? But he chose me...'

'Yes, one wonders... Have you met Rachel Vinke? Now there is a beautiful and very clever girl. I had always thought that she and Ivo would marry...'

'Probably Ivo found her too beautiful and clever,' said Serena in a sweet voice. Her companion gave her a sharp look, and then looked away from Serena's cool, calm gaze. 'And I must go and speak to Christina,' said Serena, 'and go home. The dogs need their walk.'

She offered a hand and crossed the room to where Christina was talking to two younger women, and presently, when the *burgermeester's* wife had gone, one of them asked, 'Was she cross-examining you, Serena? Don't let her worry you. She can be very unkind.'

Serena made some laughing rejoinder and said that she must go home, and went round the room saying goodbye and accepting invitations to coffee and tea and dinner parties.

It was as Christina accompanied her to the door that she said, 'Is there something wrong, Serena? Someone's been gossiping. Don't listen to it. Have you heard from Ivo?'

'Yes, he'll be home in a day or two.'

Ivo had phoned while she had been at Christina's house. He would be home on the following evening, said Wim, looking pleased.

Serena spent a restless day, which seemed endless. The *burgermeester's* wife's snide remarks refused to go away, so that she went a dozen times to a mirror to confirm her fears that she was hopelessly plain— and this Rachel was beautiful and clever, she had said. Could she be the girl she had seen Ivo with? Serena did her hair again, renewed her make-up, and took the dogs and Puss for a quite unnecessary walk.

She changed her dress after tea. Pink jersey silk— Nanny had said that Ivo liked pink. She did her hair once again and went and sat in the drawing room, the dogs at her feet, Puss curled up beside her, her knitting on her lap.

Ivo, coming quietly into the room, paused at the door. While he had been away he had thought of her constantly, and here she was, exactly as he had pictured her, sitting there, tranquil, a delight to the eye…

The next moment she had seen him, and got to her feet.

'Ivo, how nice to have you home again. Was it a success?'

He bent to kiss her cheek. 'Yes, I'm glad to say. How delightful it is to come home and find you sitting there with your knitting.'

He bent to fondle the dogs. 'Have you enjoyed your days?'

'Yes, thank you.' She gave him an account of her activities. 'And I've been in the garden with Domus; he let me help him plant out the winter pansies.'

'He did?' Ivo smiled. 'How did you manage that? He won't allow anyone to touch a blade of grass.'

'I expect it's because we can't understand a word we say to each other!'

He laughed then. 'Dinner in half an hour? I'll go and change...'

She asked questions about Madrid, and the hospital there, and the operation he had performed, and he answered her readily. But he had nothing to say about the girl who had been with him.

Serena sat wrestling with her knitting and wondered how she could find out. She could, of course, ask him, but supposing his answer was unsatisfactory? It would be best to do nothing about it. She was probably making a mountain out of a molehill. He didn't look as if he were keeping anything from her, sitting there, reading his post. She had put some invitations addressed to them both in with the pile of letters and he read them out.

'They're all from friends of mine. I see Duert and Christina have asked us for Saturday—there will be others there, of course.'

'What should I wear?'

'Something pink; you look nice in the dress you are wearing. I shall be free tomorrow afternoon; shall we go and look for something?'

'Oh, yes, please. And there's an invitation to a reception. Will that mean a long dress?'

'Oh, yes. We might see a dress we like tomorrow. Have you had any invitations to coffee, and tea parties?'

'Yes, quite a few. I went to Christina's yesterday and met several of the wives we saw at the hospital. And the *burgermeester's* wife…'

'Who no doubt peppered you with questions…?'

'Indeed she did, and a great deal of gossip. I don't think she liked me overmuch.'

He had picked up another letter and said carelessly, 'She doesn't like anyone, my dear.'

Going shopping with Ivo was much more exciting than being on her own. For one thing, she didn't need to ask the price of anything, and, for another, he was interested in what she bought. They found a deep pink dress in a silk crêpe and, since the evenings were getting chilly, a marabou stole to go over it, and while they were about it he suggested matching sandals. Serena, who would have called a halt at the dress, was enchanted. After a leisurely search around the boutiques they found a dress just right for the reception. The blue-green of a summer sea, its bodice embroidered, its taffeta skirt wide, rustling deliciously—and sandals to match, insisted Ivo, and swept her away to tea and cakes.

'Thank you, Ivo,' said Serena, choosing a rich cream cake. 'I can wear them to all the parties we will be going to. I mean, they're quite suitable for the winter.'

'My dear girl, you will need several more frocks before then. We must get some sort of a cloak for the evening too. I'm due back at the London hospital in a couple of weeks' time; would you like to come with me?'

'Yes, please. I'd like to see Nanny again, and your nice house...'

'Our nice house, Serena.'

It had been a lovely afternoon, she reflected later, watching him drive away. A private patient, he had told her, and she wasn't to wait dinner for him. He still wasn't home when she went to bed.

He was at the table when she went down to breakfast. She wished him good morning and told him not to get up, and slipped into a chair opposite him. His own good morning was absent-minded, but since he was reading his post that seemed reasonable enough to her.

She was completely taken by surprise when he said quietly, 'Dirk Veldt came to see you while I was away. Why didn't you tell me?'

He looked as calm as usual, but she had a nasty feeling that he was angry. 'Well, I really don't know, Ivo. I mean, it wasn't important. He thought I might have been lonely with you away and came to ask me to go with him for a drive in his car. I didn't want to go and I told him so. He was only here for fifteen minutes or so. I didn't invite him to stay.'

'And it was so unimportant that you didn't think to tell me of it?'

She said matter-of-factly, 'That's right. There was nothing secret about it, you know.' She added coolly, 'Husbands and wives shouldn't have secrets.' And then went slowly red, for she had a secret, hadn't she? Loving him and not saying so.

Ivo watched the telltale colour. 'I have no intention to censor your friendships, Serena. There was no reason why you shouldn't have gone for a drive with Veldt; he's an amusing companion, so I've been told.'

'I don't want to be amused,' said Serena tartly. 'Are we quarrelling?'

He laughed. 'No, no. We're both far too sensible to do that. What do you intend to do today?'

'I've been asked to have coffee with someone called Mevrouw Kasper... She's rather nice.'

'Yes, Kasper's one of the anaesthetists, a sound man. They've four children—all boys.'

'Oh, then we shall find plenty to talk about.' She buttered toast. 'Will you be home for lunch?'

'No, but in time for tea, I hope, and a long, peaceful evening.'

Mevrouw Kasper lived in Wassenaar, a leafy, wealthy suburb of Den Haag—a modern house, but not aggressively so, and roomy, with a fair-sized garden.

'We moved here,' explained Moira Kasper, pouring coffee, 'because of the boys. We needed more space.' She laughed. 'Wait till you start a family...not that that should trouble you. Ivo's house is pretty big, isn't it, and the grounds are vast.' She saw Serena's pink cheeks and added, 'Sorry, it's none of my business. How do you like living in Holland?'

'Very much, though I haven't seen a lot of it yet. We went to Friesland, to Ivo's farm there. I hope we can go again soon.'

'Perhaps now that he's married he'll take more time off—he's a glutton for work. What are you wearing to the ter Brandts' on Saturday?'

* * *

Serena enjoyed the dinner party. She knew almost everyone there, and they stood about gossiping in the ter Brandts' drawing room, drinking sherry and eating the tidbits which the three children offered. And at dinner she sat between Dr Kasper and an elderly rotund man who was quite a famous pathologist. He had a dry sense of humour, and Dr Kasper an endless fund of funny stories, so that she was happily entertained. Dirk Veldt was there, but at the other end of the table, and beyond saying hello before dinner she hadn't spoken to him. Although later, as they sat over coffee in the drawing room, he came and sat beside her for a few minutes, making polite conversation before drifting away again. Serena, aware that Ivo was watching her, made no attempt to delay him.

The pattern of her days settled into a quiet round of small chores around the house: the flowers, discussing the meals with Elly—a laborious and sometimes hilarious task, helping Domus when he was in a good mood and didn't mind her being there, taking the dogs for their walks, playing with Puss, writing longer letters to Nanny and shorter notes to her brothers, who never replied. I'm a lady of leisure if ever there was one, reflected Serena, enjoying every minute of each day, so different from her days looking after her father.

And each evening there was the joy of seeing Ivo come home, and to sit and listen while he told her about his day. She understood perhaps half of what he told her, but she stored up his remarks and spent time in the library, where she buried her head in the medical tomes there. She had started Dutch lessons too, going in to Den Haag twice a week with Ivo in the morning and spending an hour or more with a fierce little woman who worked her hard and was ruthless about homework not properly done.

And she had a busy social life now, and not all idleness, for there were various charities she had been asked to join. Life, decided Serena, was a pleasure—although not perfect. It would never be that unless Ivo discovered that he loved her, but loving him coloured her days.

The reception was to be a grand affair, and everyone she knew was going. There was a lot of talk about dresses and hairstyles, and a rumour that royalty might put in an appearance.

'I'm just a bit nervous,' she confessed to Ivo.

'No need. You will look delightful in that gown—which reminds me...'

He went out of the room and came back with two leather cases. 'The family pearls, yours now, and these earrings.' A double row of pearls with a diamond clasp and pearl earrings surrounded with diamonds.

'My goodness,' said Serena, 'They're heirlooms?'

'Yes.' He took another case from a pocket. 'And

this is a very late wedding present, Serena.' He opened the case and took out a bracelet, a delicate affair of diamonds and pearls, and fastened it onto her wrist.

'It's beautiful, Ivo,' said Serena, 'thank you.' And she kissed him. And felt him draw back. She swallowed, hurt; she must be more careful, and remember that they were friends and nothing more....

Dressed for the reception, taking a last look at herself in the pier glass, she knew that she looked almost pretty. Nothing would improve her face, of course, but her eyes were bright with excitement, her hair, in its usual simple style, had gone up well, and the dress was perfection. And, to crown everything else, the pearls and earrings and bracelet gave her an air of opulence. 'I look like a successful man's wife,' she told herself, and went downstairs to where Ivo was waiting for her.

He watched her coming carefully into the room and thought that he had never seen anyone so beautiful. He said, 'You look charming. I'm very proud of my wife, Serena.'

'Thank you—and I'm proud of you—tails do something for a man. No wonder the *burgermeester's* wife told me that you could have had any one of the beautiful and talented young women in Den Haag.'

She laughed as she spoke, and he laughed with

her. 'You will see some splendid uniforms tonight. They will probably outshine the women.'

The great hall was already crowded when they arrived. They were received by the *burgermeester* and his wife—she in purple velvet cut too tight for her ample proportions. She eyed Serena up and down before observing that she had never been able to wear that particular shade of blue-green herself, adding, 'You know many of the people here; it should be an enjoyable evening.'

Serena thanked her prettily and was swept onto the floor by Ivo. He was a good dancer, if conventional, but she was glad of that for she had had little chance to dance when she had been living at home. When the dance ended they were joined by friends and she was swept away by Duert. And after that she never lacked partners.

Her dress, she was pleased to see, was as pretty as any in the room, and that knowledge gave her an added sparkle. She was enjoying herself, and when Ivo claimed her for the supper dance she lifted a happy face to his. 'Such a lovely evening,' she told him.

Soon to be spoilt.

Leaving the supper room presently, they came face to face with the *burgermeester* and his wife, and with them was a young woman. Serena recognised her at once—she had been with Ivo at the hospital and in his car. And now, having a closer look, she could see that she was strikingly beautiful, with almost black hair and large dark eyes. She was dressed in black, something slinky and soft, showing off her splendid figure.

And Ivo had stopped, so that Serena had to stop too.

'You must meet,' said the *burgermeester's* wife. 'Ivo must have mentioned Rachel to you, Serena— such old friends.' She smiled maliciously. 'Serena, this is Rachel Vinke. Serena is Ivo's wife.'

She watched them both with sharp eyes and Serena offered a hand, somehow managing to keep a smile on her face. 'How nice to meet you,' she said, and was pleased to hear how friendly she sounded. Rachel shook hands, murmured something conventional and turned to Ivo.

'Ivo, we must talk; there is a great deal I have to say to you.'

She flashed a smiling look at Serena. 'You do not mind? A personal matter, you understand?' She turned back to Ivo. 'Tomorrow, perhaps? If I come to the hospital?' She frowned. 'No, of course it will be Sunday…'

'Why not come to lunch?' asked Serena, surprised at the words which had popped out of her mouth before she could stop them. She had been mad to utter them, but at least she had seen the disconcerted look on the *burgermeester's* lady's face. When she glanced at Ivo there was no way of knowing if he was pleased or not; he looked exactly the same as always: calm and remote and pleasant.

'That would be ideal,' said Rachel. 'We will then have the leisure to talk, you and I?'

Ivo's voice was giving nothing away; he agreed with just the right amount of interest expected of him, and after a few minutes' talk they separated.

Serena, not sure what was to happen next, said quickly, 'I'm going to tidy myself before the dancing starts again,' whisked herself away. She wasn't certain, but she had the feeling that Ivo was angry.

And so he might well be, she thought angrily, pinning her already tidy hair, springing a surprise like that on her just when she was enjoying herself. Well, he couldn't say that she was interfering in his life like a possessive wife. They were friends and nothing more, weren't they? She whirled herself back to the ballroom, and the first thing she saw was Ivo with Rachel. She was looking up at him as they danced, and talking... The second was Dirk Veldt, who swung her onto the floor before she had the chance to speak.

'I was beginning to think that I would never get the chance to dance with you,' he told her, 'but I see Ivo is engrossed with Rachel Vinke. You've met her?

She's beautiful, isn't she? Personally I prefer your type of beauty, Serena. You look gorgeous tonight.'

She didn't believe that, of course, but it was welcoming to her unhappy ears. He was holding her too tightly, but she didn't care. If Ivo could go dancing off with this Rachel who seemed to know him so well, she had every right to dance with Dirk. And what did they want to talk about? Something that necessitated her coming to lunch....

'You're not listening to a word I'm saying,' said Dirk, bending his head to speak softly into her ear.

She wasn't, but as Ivo and Rachel were close enough to see them, Serena gave Dirk a brilliant smile.

The dancing went on for some time. She had partners for all the dances, and two more with Dirk, but at last it was the final dance and Ivo claimed her. They danced in silence, and when it finally ended they made their way back out of the ballroom, stopping to speak to friends as they went.

Ivo said, 'I will wait here while you get your coat.' He spoke pleasantly, but his eyes were cold. She had made him angry and she told herself that she was glad of it. If he wanted to quarrel she was quite willing...

In the car, beside him, she said defiantly, 'What a delightful evening. I did enjoy it. Didn't you, Ivo?' She added daringly, 'Meeting so many people too.'

He gave a grunt and didn't speak again until they were home. In the hall, Serena yawned. 'There's coffee on the Aga if you want some, Ivo. I think I'll go straight to bed.' She turned as she reached the staircase. 'Goodnight Ivo.'

He was standing in the hall, looking at her. 'You danced a good deal with Veldt.' He spoke very quietly.

'Yes.' It seemed prudent to start climbing the staircase. 'He's a good dancer and great fun...'

'Were you paying me back in my own coin, Serena?' he asked blandly.

'As a matter of fact I was. What's sauce for the goose is sauce for the gander.'

The look on his face didn't exactly frighten her, but it sent her running up to her room at a fine rate.

By the morning's light she regretted every word she had said. Never mind that he had hurt her so that she actually ached with unhappiness. When they had married they had struck a bargain; she had known exactly what he had wanted and she had agreed to it—a calm partnership with no pretence of love, only friendship and liking and a comfortable knowing that they got on well together. And now she had shattered that.

She got up and dressed and went down to breakfast, and found him standing by the open door. The dogs were in the garden and Puss was sitting by his feet.

He turned to wish her a genial good morning and she said at once, 'Oh, don't be nice, Ivo. I'm sorry— I shouldn't have said what I did last night. If you want to be angry I'll deserve every word of it. And I only danced with Dirk Veldt to annoy you...'

He turned from the door as the dogs came in. 'My dear, Serena, why should I be angry? You may dance with whom you choose and say what you wish.'

'Yes, that's all very well, but that isn't what we agreed, is it? We were to have a friendly marriage and not—not interfere. And you have every right to see your friends. She's very beautiful...'

'Ah,' said Ivo, in such a strange voice that she looked at him again.

'You believe that I am enjoying the resumption of a love affair?' he went on bitingly. 'We have been married a matter of a few weeks, Serena. If that is what you think of me then perhaps we should confine our feelings to the friendship to which you so often allude and avoid looking too closely at each other's lives.'

'Oh, Ivo,' said Serena miserably.

'Shall we have breakfast? It's a splendid morning for a walk, and you can tell me what you thought of the reception.'

He sounded his usual calm self again; the whole unfortunate episode was to be overlooked. Now she would never know about Rachel Vinke...

CHAPTER EIGHT

IT WAS still early when they started out with the dogs, and Serena, anxious to make amends, said, 'We mustn't be too long. I don't know at what time Juffrouw Vinke is coming. I told Elly there would be a guest for lunch—it's duckling and cherry sauce, but there's one of Elly's raised pies in case she doesn't like duckling. And Domus let me have some strawberries from the greenhouse.'

She fell silent, aware that she was babbling, and Ivo said, 'Rachel is married. I said I would fetch her around noon. How are you getting on with your Dutch lessons?'

It was a gentle snub; she had deserved it, she supposed. 'Very well, I think, though the grammar is puzzling and I quite often miss out on the verbs —I mean, having to tack them onto the end of a sentence, one tends to overlook them.'

'Well, you will have a short respite soon. I'm due at the hospital in London in just over a week. I have to go to Leeds too, but you will be happy with Nanny?'

'Oh, yes, it will be lovely to see her again. I must find something to take her.' She glanced at her watch. 'Shouldn't we be turning back? If you're going to fetch Mevrouw Vinke...'

He took her arm as they retraced their steps. 'You are anxious to meet Rachel again? I don't imagine that you have much in common.'

'We're both women,' said Serena, and heard his rumble of laughter.

Waiting for Ivo to come with their guest, Serena wandered around the drawing room, peering in the mirror beneath the windows, poking at her hair, putting on more lipstick and then rubbing it off again. A waste of time, she told herself. She had no hope of competing with someone as beautiful as Rachel.

She told herself how right she had been as she went to welcome Rachel as she got out of the car—in white from head to toe. The simplicity of her dress owed its art to couture, and made Serena's straw-coloured linen two-piece insignificant. And her make-up was faultless...

Serena, very aware of her own shortcomings, greeted her with the social smile she had learnt, to cover her true feelings.

'Such a lovely day,' she observed. 'Do come in. What can we get you to drink?'

They had their drinks sitting by the window overlooking the ornamental pool at the back of the house, and Serena made small talk and didn't look at Ivo. He was, as he always was, a perfect host, and it was impossible to tell from his manner whether Rachel was just a friend or someone much nearer than that. And over lunch Serena had to admit to herself that she quite liked Rachel; she was amusing and a good talker, and she had a warm and ready smile. And she was attractive…

As they finished their coffee, Rachel said, 'And now I must talk to you, Ivo. Serena does not mind?'

'Not a bit.' Serena summoned the smile again. 'I'll take the dogs for a run. You'll stay for tea?'

'I would have liked that, but I have a plane to catch…'

She watched them go to Ivo's study and whistled to the dogs. How long would they be? she wondered. And then set off at a brisk pace, trying to forget about them. But she was back in the house an hour later, sitting in the drawing room, her ears stretched to hear the study door open.

They came into the drawing room presently; Ivo's face showed no more than its usual calm, and Rachel was smiling widely.

'That is all settled,' she told Serena. 'And now I must go back to my dear Jan. He will be so relieved that everything is settled. I don't know what we would have done without Ivo's help, first to put together his broken arms and legs and then to deal with all this tiresome lawsuit. But now at last it is—how do you say?—plain sailing.'

But not for Serena, of course. She asked, 'Your husband—he has been hurt in an accident?'

'Ivo did not tell you? A car crash—not his fault. He has broken both his legs and both his arms. Can you imagine anything more terrible? And Ivo has put him together again. We knew he would, and he came to Madrid at once when I came to ask him—he and Jan are old friends, you see. And then he has arranged everything with Jan's solicitors—it is to go to court, you see. Today I brought the last of the papers for Ivo to see and sign.'

She flashed Serena a brilliant smile. 'It is so like Ivo to do all this and say nothing.'

She kissed Serena warmly. 'When Jan is well again you must both come and stay with us. And now I must go, but I am glad that I have met you. You are just as Ivo described you.'

Ivo had been standing at the window with his back to them. Now he turned round to say, 'We had better leave, Rachel, we're cutting it fine.'

He looked at Serena then. 'I should be back before dinner.'

He touched her shoulder as they went out, but he didn't kiss her.

By the time he returned Serena was in a bad temper. He had deliberately misled her; there had been no reason why he couldn't have explained about Rachel. Perhaps he had found it amusing. She ground her splendid teeth and tossed back a glass of sherry that she didn't want.

The moment he came through the door she rounded on him, made reckless by a second glass of sherry and a strong sense of grievance.

'You could have told me.' Her voice was shrill, so she paused and started again. 'About Rachel. It was beastly of you to let me think the things I did.'

'And what did you think, Serena? Or shall we ignore your regrettable thoughts? And I didn't tell you for the simple reason that you had already drawn your own conclusions.'

He had crossed the room and come to stand before her, and suddenly gave a chuckle. 'You've been at the sherry…'

Which was just too much for her. 'I hate you,' said Serena in a choked voice, and raced out of the room and upstairs, where she banged her bedroom door shut, flung herself on the bed and burst into tears.

Ivo stood for a while, looking at nothing and deep in thought. He had the look of a man who had made a delightful discovery. Presently he went to his dinner, requesting Wim to make sure that *mevrouw* should have a supper tray taken to her bedroom.

'She has a severe headache,' he told his elderly retainer, who went to the kitchen and told Elly that he was willing to bet his week's wages on the master and missus being not on speaking terms for the moment.

'It'll blow over,' said Elly. 'Look at the times you and me have had words, and here we are after I don't know how many years.'

Wim took the supper tray from her and kissed her plump cheek. 'Forty next year,' he told her, and trod carefully upstairs to tap on Serena's door.

It was perhaps not very romantic to be hungry when one's heart was breaking, but Serena polished off the contents of the tray and then, since there was nothing else to do and she had no intention of going back to the drawing room, lay in a hot bath until she was as pink as a lobster and went to bed. Where, rather to her surprise, she fell asleep at once.

The thought of facing Ivo across the breakfast table was daunting, but she wasn't a coward, and dressed in a patterned skirt and a cashmere top, she went downstairs.

Ivo came in from the garden as she reached the breakfast table. His good morning was friendly, as was his enquiry as to her headache. 'You slept well?'

'Like a log,' said Serena, 'and I didn't have a headache, only a bad temper!'

He passed her the toast. 'One of the things I like about you, my dear, is your honesty, so perhaps you will set my mind at rest about something you said. That you hated me...'

He was staring at her across the table, not smiling, but not angry either.

'No, I don't hate you,' she said. 'I'm sorry I said that, but I was cross.'

He smiled at her. 'So you were…'

'Are you never cross, Ivo? I mean wanting to shout at someone?'

'Not cross, but angry. Yes, I can be angry, but self-control is something one learns quite quickly in the medical profession. I'll be home for lunch and I have to visit an old patient in the afternoon. Would you like to come with me?'

'Oh, yes, I would. In Den Haag?'

'No—an old lady who lives in Leiden.' He was sitting back in his chair and Puss jumped onto his knees, ignoring the dogs at his feet. He looked the picture of a happily married man. Something which he confidently expected to be, given the patience to wait for Serena to discover that she was a happily married woman…

They were back on their old friendly footing, thought Serena, happily going to the kitchen to discuss the day's meals with Elly.

Her Dutch was improving. She knew the names of their foods now, and could add a few words to them, and Elly never smiled at her accent or her mistakes so that her morning visit was a pleasure. And, that settled, she took the dogs for their walk and went back presently to write a letter to Nanny with Puss curled on her lap.

It was a short drive to Leiden—ten miles or so—and since they were on the motorway there wasn't much to see, but when they reached Leiden Serena found plenty to look at and admire. When Ivo stopped in a narrow street beside a canal, with a row of small gabled houses facing it, she exclaimed with delight. The houses were indeed old, leaning against each other, each gable different. They presented a pristine appearance, with shining paintwork and gleaming windows.

She crossed the cobbles with Ivo and stood beside him as he banged the heavy doorknocker, which was opened almost immediately by a stout woman with screwed up grey hair and very bright blue eyes. She broke into speech when she saw Ivo, shook hands with them both and ushered them inside.

The hall was tiny, with a steep, narrow staircase facing the door and a half-open door to one side. The room beyond was small and crowded with furniture, and every flat surface was covered by photo frames and china ornaments. And sitting in the middle of it was a very small old lady, dressed severely in black. She had a round face and small dark eyes, a little beaky nose and white hair, piled high.

Ivo went to kiss her cheek and then introduced

Serena, who shook a hand as thin and light as a bird's claw and murmured a greeting in her careful Dutch. The old lady looked her up and down and had a great deal to say to Ivo. Whatever it was made him laugh, and he drew a chair forward for Serena. 'Mevrouw Boldt says you are as pretty as a picture, Serena. You will not mind if we speak Dutch? I must ask her questions about her health. She worked for my mother years ago, and had an accident recently and broke her leg and hip. I just need to check them.'

So Serena sat quietly, listening to Ivo's quiet voice, watching his calm face, wondering if he would ever love her. And presently the woman who had admitted them came in with a tea tray. The china cups and saucers were very small, and the tea was weak, without milk or sugar, but there was a plate of little sugary biscuits. Serena sipped her tea, making it last, and nibbled a biscuit. She had a nasty feeling that there wouldn't be second cups and she was right.

Ivo had finished his talk with Mevrouw Boldt, and the conversation became general, with Serena's faltering Dutch smoothly helped out by Ivo, who translated the old lady's questions to her and popped in the right word when Serena got stuck with her replies. But the old lady seemed to like her, and when they got up to go she was invited to kiss the paper-thin cheek.

'You are to come with me again,' said Ivo, bidding the woman who had admitted them goodbye.

In the car he said, 'Mevrouw Boldt is over eighty, but she lives in the manner of her youth and has no intention of changing her ways. She was with my parents for more than fifty years and retired here with her husband, who was our gardener. Until she fell and broke a hip a year or so ago she was very active.'

'So you keep an eye on her?'

'Yes. You liked her little house?'

'It's charming—rather a lot of furniture and ornaments...'

'Her possessions, much treasured.'

'Do you visit her often?'

'As often as I can. You'll come with me again?'

'Yes, please. And perhaps by then my Dutch will be better.'

'You do very well, Serena.' He turned to smile at her and she smiled back, just for the moment happy.

They went to England soon after that, and although Serena was glad to be seeing Nanny once more, she hated leaving the dogs and Puss; she hated leaving the lovely old house too, and her friends.

'The change will do you good,' said Christina, 'and you can do some shopping for me.'

Ivo took the car, since he had to go to Leeds as

well as London, and they crossed from the Hoek and
then drove from Harwich.

It was nice to be in England again, reflected Serena, though at the same time she wished that they
were back in Holland. But Nanny's welcome was so
warm that she forgot that for the moment. The little
mews cottage offered a cosy welcome, and London
could look delightful on a fine day.

Ivo went at once to the hospital, leaving her to
gossip with Nanny and unpack, and she didn't see
him again until the evening. Over dinner he told her
that he would be at the hospital all day. 'Have you
any plans?' he wanted to know. 'I'm sorry to leave
you on the first day...'

'I'm going shopping,' said Serena, 'for Christina
and for me. Do you want anything?'

'No, thanks. I'll try and get tickets for the theatre.
What would you like to see?'

They decided on a musical. 'And we might have
a night out after I get back from Leeds.'

She realised after the first day that she wasn't going to see much of him. It wasn't just his operating
lists at the hospital, there were clinics, and on several
evenings meetings with his colleagues. But at least
she saw him at breakfast, and for dinner in the evening. And they had their evening at the theatre. When
she had been living at home no one had taken her to
the theatre—indeed, no one had taken her anywhere.

The visit to the theatre was a treat, and she enjoyed it with the whole- hearted delight of a child. Ivo, watching her rapt face, saw almost nothing of the show.

It was on the next day that he went to Leeds. He would be gone for three days, he told her, dropping a light kiss on her cheek, getting into his car and driving away.

Serena smiled and waved, and then went up to her room and had a good cry. She wasn't sure why she cried, but she felt better for it, and after mopping her face and putting on fresh make-up she went in search of Nanny. They would go shopping, she insisted. She needed several things, and surely Nanny too had things to buy?

And Nanny, taking a look at Serena's pink nose, agreed immediately.

They spent most of the day at Harrods, where Nanny expressed astonishment at the prevailing fashions and then spent happy hours in the food hall. Serena bought sweets for Christina's children, and a very beautiful scarf for Christina, and then searched for suitable gifts to take to Wim and Elly and the rest of the staff. And for old Domus she found a lavender bush, small enough to go in the car.

They went back home, tired but pleased with their efforts, and for her part Serena was glad that one day away from Ivo was already nearly over.

She and Nanny were in the kitchen when he came home. Nanny was making cakes and Serena was sitting on the kitchen table, running a finger round the remains of the cake mixture in the bowl. She was sampling it from one finger when he walked in.

She was off the table and running to meet him when she remembered that he might not like such a display of delight. She came to a halt before him and changed the happy grin on her face to one of friendly surprise.

'Ivo, how nice you're back. Did you have a good trip? Do you want a meal? Tea won't be for another hour, but we can get you a meal straight away.'

Ivo didn't kiss her because he wasn't sure if he could trust himself to stop at a peck on her cheek. He said in his quiet voice, 'Hello, Serena—Nanny. I'll wait for tea; I had a meal before I left. I must do some phoning and catch up on my post; I'll join you in an hour.'

He smiled at them and went out of the kitchen, then crossed the hall to his study and shut the door.

And that's how it will always be, reflected Serena unhappily, doors shut in my face, however gently. She helped Nanny tidy the kitchen and then went to the drawing room. A good thing she had brought her knitting with her; she plunged into it now, glad it was complicated, and that it needed her concentration and the counting of stitches.

So when Ivo came into the room there she was, sitting, to all intents and purposes, perfectly composed, looking up at him with the kind of smile a long-married wife might give her husband.

Ivo sat down opposite to her, studying her ordinary face and neat head of hair. She was, he considered, not only pretty—very pretty—she was the epitome of what every wife should be. She might not have loved him when they married, but from time to time—in the kitchen just now, he reflected—her behaviour made him hope that in time she would love him. He must have patience, he reflected, let her find her feet in this new life she was leading.

'Did you go shopping?' he asked.

'Yes, with Nanny. We had a lovely day, drooling round the Harrods food hall.' She added, 'And I bought two dresses—they were so pretty—and I'm sure I'll have a chance to wear them later on.'

'Before then. Would you like to dine out tomorrow evening? And I thought we might go dancing on Saturday night.' He smiled at her. 'A chance to wear those frocks.'

He took her to the Ritz, where, in one of the new dresses, she dined off jellied lobster, spinach and walnut salad, rump of lamb and a dessert of fruit, cream and ice cream which beggared description. Over coffee Serena said happily, 'This is a heavenly place. Do you come here often?'

Ivo smiled. 'No, only on very special occasions.'

'Oh, is this a special occasion?'

'I think we should make it one, don't you?'

She wasn't sure if he was serious or not. She looked out of the window to the park beyond and then, struck by a sudden thought said, 'Is it your birthday? I ought to know when it is, oughtn't I? If it is…'

'No, no, don't worry. We shall be going back home in two days' time. I've a meeting tomorrow evening, but we might go to Claridge's on the following evening. Would you like that?'

Serena beamed at him across the table. 'Oh, yes, I would. Is it as splendid as this?'

'Just about. Are you tired?'

'Tired? Heavens, no… But you've had a busy day, haven't you? It's been lovely, but I'm ready to go home if you would like that.'

'No, no. I'm not in the least tired. I wondered if you would like to walk. We'll take the car as far as the Embankment.'

It was a lovely night: moon and stars and cold enough for her to pull her soft coat around her shoulders. And the Embankment was the best possible place to be, she decided, with the lights reflected on the Thames and the hundreds of lights from the city's windows. They strolled arm-in-arm, not always talking, but happy in their silences. Serena's head was empty of thoughts; it was filled with content. This could go on for ever, she reflected, only of course it wouldn't! But just for the moment life was perfect.

They went back to the car later, and drove home and sat in the kitchen drinking the coffee Nanny had left on the Aga. And when she got up to go to bed, Serena kissed Ivo's cheek shyly, not sure if he minded that.

'It was a lovely evening, thank you, Ivo. And I look forward to going to Claridge's. Do you have to leave early in the morning?'

'Yes. I've a list at eight o'clock, but I should be home for tea.'

He stood looking down at her, waiting for her to go through the door he was holding open for her. The perfume she wore was faint but fragrant, and he dropped a quick kiss on the top of her neat head of hair as she passed him, so light that she didn't feel it.

She did the shopping for Nanny in the morning, and after they had had their lunch together took herself for a brisk walk. Ivo would be home for tea and they would have their evening together. She smiled widely at the thought so that passers-by stared at her happy face.

It was while they were having their tea that she remembered that he had a meeting that evening.

'When would you like dinner?' she wanted to know.

'Did I forget to tell you? I'm sorry, I'm dining with some of the committee members before the meeting starts.' He glanced at his watch. 'I'd better go and change.'

'I expect you'll be back late?'

'Probably.' He saw her downcast face. 'Don't wait up, my dear, I'll see you at breakfast.'

She bade him goodbye cheerfully enough; she had heaps of things to do, she assured him, and she must start sorting out things ready to pack.

Ivo nodded absently, his mind already on the meeting ahead.

But he made up for his absence by taking her to Claridge's, as he had promised. As sumptuous a restaurant as the Ritz, Serena decided. There wasn't a pin to choose between them, and the food was just as delicious. And to crown the evening's pleasure they danced into the small hours. When at length she got to bed she was too sleepy to think sensibly, but it had been another evening to remember for life.

Serena was sorry to say goodbye to Nanny, although, as Ivo pointed out, it was only a matter of a few hours' journey for her to return whenever she wanted to.

'You'll be coming again?'

'Certainly, in a couple of months' time. I may

come over for brief visits—spend one night, perhaps.'

He gave Nanny a hug, popped Serena into the car and drove off. On the way to Harwich he asked, 'Did you phone your brothers? Would you like to visit them? Now that we are married and settled down they may feel differently about us.'

Serena thought that even if Ivo had settled down she hadn't. She peeped at his calm profile. 'I phoned them, but they were still annoyed; I don't think I'd better visit them yet.'

Henry had been nasty, as only Henry could be, and Matthew had talked to her as though she had disgraced the whole family. She said, 'Gregory has married. She's the daughter of the Mayor of Yeovil. He must be glad he gave me up!'

Ivo's hand came down on her knees. 'I'm the one who is glad,' he told her.

The crossing was smooth, and they were back home in time to eat the light supper Wim had ready for them. Ivo would be going to the hospital in the morning, so he excused himself with the plea of letters to read, phone calls to make and the dogs to take for a walk. Serena, mindful of her wish to be the perfect wife, bade him goodnight and went up to her lovely room with Puss and unpacked and bathed and got into bed. She was lonely. She supposed that loving someone and not being able to tell them that made for loneliness. She lay awake for a long time, until she heard Ivo come to bed well past midnight.

Life had settled down into its quiet pattern again.

She went to see Christina the next day, handed over the things she had bought for her, agreed to sell flags for a charity, to help at a bazaar in aid of orphans and attend a concert in which Christina's children were appearing, and then on an impulse she took a tram to Scheveningen, where she walked along the promenade until she was tired. There were plenty of people and a great many children playing on the sands. She took the tram back in a while, and went back home to eat her solitary lunch and take the dogs for a walk.

When Ivo got home after tea she was in the drawing room, knitting the second sleeve of the sweater. She was rather tired of it by now, and probably Ivo wouldn't like it. She decided that she would start on a set of tapestry covers for the dining room chairs. The work of a lifetime...

Several days later she went into Den Haag, collected her flags and collecting box and went to her allotted pitch outside a bookshop, which pleased her since she could from time to time study all the latest editions in its windows. The street was a busy one, and she rattled her box with a will, smiling at the passers-by whether they stopped or not. She was enjoying herself; it was a fine winter's morning and she liked the bustle around her, and later on she would meet Christina for lunch and compare notes...

The morning was well advanced when Dirk Veldt stopped in front of her.

'Serena, how delightful to see you, and what a marvellous excuse to stop and chat while you sell me one of these flags.'

She offered him a flag. 'Shouldn't you be working at the hospital?'

'A man must eat; I'm taking a long lunch hour.' He gave her a charming smile. 'Will you share it with me? There's a little restaurant near here where they serve the most delicious sole baked in cream...'

'No, thank you, Dirk. I'm here for another hour and then I'm lunching with Christina ter Brandt. You haven't given me any money for your flag.'

He shrugged, and fished in his pocket for a note. 'I shan't give up. You must be exciting under that matter-of-fact manner.'

'Well, you're wrong, and do go away. Enjoy that sole. Perhaps you'll find a pretty girl you can share it with.'

She smiled at him, wishing that he would go. And Ivo, driving to his consulting rooms, saw the smile. The rage which engulfed him needed all his self-control to subdue.

It was late afternoon when he got home and Serena, very satisfied with her efforts, was in the drawing room, the tea tray beside her.

She looked up as he went in, gave him a smiling greeting and asked if he would like tea. 'It's a bit late,' she explained, 'but I had lunch with Christina and we sat talking. I sold all my flags too.'

Ivo sat down, refused her offer of tea, and enquired idly if she had enjoyed herself.

'Yes, I did, and people were very generous.' She went rather pink. 'Dirk Veldt bought a flag from me. He wanted me to have lunch with him.'

And Ivo sighed with relief—she had told him of her own free will...

'And why didn't you? He's an amusing companion, I should imagine.'

The pink deepened. 'I thought I liked him when I met him. I mean, I didn't know anyone, and he came and talked to me and made me feel that I was someone—if you see what I mean? You see, Ivo, I never had much of a social life, and I know I'm a plain Jane but he made me feel pretty. But now I have friends, and I go to committee meetings and bazaars and things like that. I've found my feet.' She stopped to think. 'And now I know that I don't like him. We're bound to meet, aren't we? But he doesn't have to be a friend.'

Ivo listened to this with deep satisfaction. His Serena had indeed found her feet; she was happy and busy and she was liked by everyone who met her. And he had glimpsed the look of delight on her face when he had come into the room. Perhaps now was the right time…

'Serena…'

The phone stopped him. He picked it up and she listened to his quiet voice saying little. She knew enough Dutch now to understand that it was urgent, and when he put the phone down and told her that he must return to the hospital for an emergency operation, she said, 'Hard luck, Ivo. We'll wait dinner for you. It's something that'll keep. I hope it's successful, whatever you will have to do.'

She smiled at him as he paused by her chair to kiss her cheek, and she wondered what it was that he had been going to say to her.

He phoned from the hospital later on that evening; he would be late home. Would she ask Elly to leave something on the Aga for him? He would see her at breakfast.

She knew better than to waste his time asking questions. In the morning at breakfast he might tell her about it. It pleased her that he was getting into the habit of describing his work to her, and she still spent hours in the library looking up the long words that he used so that she could look intelligent.

She wrote letters after dinner, a long, newsy one to Nanny and dutiful ones to her brothers, and by the time she had finished it was almost eleven o'clock. She went upstairs to bed and then, suddenly making up her mind, went down the stairs again in her dressing gown to find Wim. She would stay up, she told him. He was to go to bed after he had locked up. Ivo had his key, and once he was home he would bolt the door after him.

Wim demurred. The master would probably be very late, he told her, and she would lose her sleep. But she persuaded him at last, and he went round securing the doors and windows, settling the dogs in their baskets and turning out all but the lights in the hall and the kitchen.

'For that's where I shall sit,' declared Serena. 'I can ready Elly's cookbooks and keep an eye on whatever it is that she has left on the Aga.'

The kitchen was warm and quiet. The *stoelklok* by the dresser tick-tocked with soothing monotony, the dogs snored gently and Puss had curled up on her lap. It was a very cosy room, despite its size; it smelled of baking and coffee, mingled with a whiff of something tasty keeping warm in the oven. Serena sat contentedly, patiently waiting. She wasn't sleepy, and Ivo might like to mull over his work at the hospital.

She had been there for an hour or more when he came in, to stop short in the doorway as he saw her.

She put Puss down gently and got out of her chair.

'I wasn't sleepy, so I thought I'd wait for you. There's something in the oven, and coffee. Did things go well?'

He came slowly into the room. 'Yes, as far as we can tell at the moment. There was no need for you to wait up, Serena.'

'But you must eat something…'

'I had something at the hospital. Go to bed, my dear. I must just go to the study to check something, and then I shall go up myself…'

He was holding the door open for her. It was obvious that he didn't want her company. She summoned a smile. 'Well, the coffee's hot if you should change your mind,' she told him cheerfully. 'Goodnight, Ivo.'

That had been a mistake, she told herself, taking no notice of the tears trickling down her cheeks. She must remember never to do that again.

CHAPTER NINE

IT SEEMED to Serena that Ivo was avoiding her. Unless he had been called away early they breakfasted together, and either dined at home or with friends. They walked the dogs, went to an occasional theatre, but although he was a pleasant and thoughtful companion she sensed a reserve in his manner, and never once did he talk about them. She decided that no woman could feel less married than she did, and that something must be done about it. There was always some reason why he had to go to his study after dinner, or return to the hospital until the late evening. And of course when they dined with friends they had no chance to talk...

The plain unhappy fact was that he didn't enjoy her company. And yet when they had married he had made it very clear that he liked her well enough to marry her. Rachel was no longer a threat, but perhaps there was someone else? He was a man any girl would want to attract... She squashed the thought as unworthy. Perhaps there was something about her which annoyed him? And the best way to find out would be to ask him.

She chose to do it one evening when, after half an

hour or so together in the drawing room after dinner, Ivo put down the newspaper he was reading.

'I've some notes to look through…'

'Before you go there's something I want to ask you,' said Serena, and now that she had got the words out she wished that she hadn't spoken, because the look he gave her was suddenly intent.

'Yes?'

She must have been mistaken about the look; his voice was as mild as milk. She put down her knitting and met his look.

'There's something not right,' she began. 'Have I done something which has annoyed you? Am I too dull? Perhaps I don't behave as I should when we go out, or wear the wrong clothes. Whatever it is I wish you would tell me and I'll put it right.' She added in a voice which had become a little sharp, 'I think you are avoiding me. Oh, not just being with me, I mean when we're together you're remote.' She sighed. 'I'm not explaining very well, am I?' And when he didn't speak she added carefully, 'I don't want to intrude on your life. That was partly why you married me, wasn't it? To be a friend and a companion but not a real wife. And I thought it was working out very well.'

'Tell me, Serena, are you quite content with our marriage?'

He showed no signs of anger, only interest.

Serena longed to shout No at him. How could she be content when she loved him so much? Faced with the years ahead and never being allowed to tell him. Instead she said, 'Yes, I am,' and went rather red because she didn't lie easily.

Ivo got out of his chair and stood in front of her chair, towering over her so that she had to crane her neck to look at him.

He was smiling. 'Well, I'm not…' And the phone rang.

Ivo van Doelen wasn't a man who swore habitually, but now he let out a robust Dutch oath which fortunately Serena didn't understand, but his voice was quiet as he answered it, listened, replied briefly. He said, 'I must go at once,' and was out of the room before she could open her mouth.

She would wait up for him, she decided. He might be back within an hour or so. Now that she had broken the ice they could talk—at least she could do the talking. She wasn't sure if he had been listening, for all he had done was ask if she were content…

But when the *stoelklok* chimed eleven she gave up the idea; he would be too tired to listen, too tired to talk. She went up to bed; perhaps in the morning she would try again…

But she saw at once when she went down to breakfast that it was out of the question. Ivo was as immaculate as always, but there were tired lines in his face.

'Did you get any sleep?' she asked him, after wishing him a good morning.

'A couple of hours. I didn't disturb you when I came in?'

He was his usual friendly self, passing her the toast, commenting on the weather.

'No. Have you a busy day? You couldn't take a few hours off?'

'I'm afraid not. I've a clinic this morning, and I'm operating at Leiden this afternoon.'

He gathered up his post and got up from the table. 'I should be home around teatime.'

He laid a hand on her shoulder as he passed by her chair. 'Enjoy your day.'

Which of course she didn't; she worried until she had a headache.

A few hours in the garden with Domus made her feel better. They still didn't understand what the other was saying, but somehow they managed to work together, she undertaking the humbler tasks of weeding and thinning seedlings while he did complicated jobs such as grafting and pruning. She felt so much better that she went indoors and spent a long time learning her next lesson for her visit to her teacher on the following day. And when Christina phoned to ask her if she and Ivo were going to the *burgermeester's* dinner party she was so bright and chatty that Christina put down the phone wondering why Serena sounded so unlike herself.

Ivo thought the same thing when he got home. Serena, usually so quiet and restful, talked non-stop, barely giving him time to answer or make any comment, and although she asked him about his day, she gave him no chance to answer. Any ideas he had had about a serious talk he rejected, for Serena was clearly not in the mood.

And so it was for the next few days; Serena was hiding behind a barrier of small talk. She was friendly, made sure that his house was run exactly as he wished, was a charming hostess when he brought colleagues back with him one afternoon but the barrier was there, as intractable as barbed wire.

They just couldn't go on like it, of course; he would be free on the following weekend and he would tell her that it was impossible to go on as they were. His hope that she might learn to love him was fading fast, but he would tell her that he loved her, even if it meant that she would want to end their marriage. That she was unhappy about it seemed evident to him. It was such a pity that each time they had been on the point of talking about it they had been interrupted.

But nothing of their disquiet showed when they reached the *burgermeester's* house; they appeared to be exactly what they were: a newly married couple and very happy. Only Christina saw the dark circles under Serena's eyes and Ivo's bland expression which concealed his true feelings.

'There's something wrong,' she told Duert as they were getting ready to go to bed. 'I have a feeling in my bones…'

'Well, don't try and find out, my darling, it might make matters worse. Allow Fate to settle the matter in her own way; she always does.'

And he was right.

Several days passed, and Serena wondered uneasily if she would get a chance to talk to Ivo. He was busier than ever, it seemed, sometimes away overnight, often late home in the evening. He was invariably pleasant, enquiring after her days, her Dutch lessons, whether she had heard from Nanny…but there was never time to do more than give him a quick answer.

He was going to Luxembourg in the morning, he told her one evening. To operate on one of its leading citizens. 'Nothing too serious. If all goes well I should be home late in the evening, or at least the following morning. I'll phone you as soon as I know.'

He had gone with a quick peck on her cheek and a wish that she would have a pleasant day.

He phoned in the early evening. He would have

to stay longer than he had expected. He would be home some time during the following evening.

Serena went to bed early, which was silly because she didn't sleep until early morning, and woke wondering how to fill the empty day stretching endlessly until Ivo should be home again. She would go to the sea, she decided, and got up to an early breakfast, took the dogs for their walk and went home to find a message from Christina. Would she go to the new day centre that had been opened in Den Haag? A project to keep young people with nothing to do off the streets. There was to be a free meal at midday, and they were short of helpers.

Serena agreed at once, and went in search of Wim. She explained that she would be out for most of the day and asked him to drive her to the centre.

Wim didn't approve. The centre was in a poor quarter of the city; he wasn't sure if the master would approve either.

'There will be several ladies there, Wim,' Serena assured him, 'and I'll be back around teatime.'

She had to agree with him about the shabbiness of the centre's surroundings: mean streets with small houses, many of them with their windows boarded up.

Wim tut-tutted with disapproval. 'There are illegal immigrants here from all over Europe. They bring many children with them and there is not always any work.'

He was reassured to see several ladies going to and fro inside the centre, and Serena said briskly, 'You see, Wim, there are any number of us here. And I'll get a lift back.'

She was given an apron the moment she put her face round the door, and the *burgermeester's* wife— in charge, of course—directed her to one of the long counters set up in the main room. And no sooner was Serena behind it when the doors were opened and people poured in. A medley of humanity, not just the young people she had expected, but the old, and mothers with young children. She poured soup and handed bread and mugs of coffee, hoping she was doing the right thing, for there was no chance of talking to any of the other helpers.

It was a seemingly unending stream, and she was quite sure that several of the younger ones came back for second helpings. And while the food held out, why not? she asked herself. When the *burgermeester's* wife came round to make sure that everyone was doing things the right way, and told her that on no account must she allow anyone to have more than one helping, Serena replied with suitable meekness and doled out more soup to a very large and hungry-looking man who undoubtedly needed it.

The lady helpers were supposed to leave their positions in turn, in order to refresh themselves with coffee in a back room, but somehow Serena didn't manage to get there. The food and soup were beginning to run out and the afternoon was well advanced. The crowd was thinning, although there were still a great many young mothers with babies and toddlers.

After this, the opening day, marked by the free lunch, the centre would cater only for schoolchildren and teenagers, and the old people and small children would stand no chance. Serena scraped out the soup to the last drop and handed out the last of the bread. The coffee had long since gone.

The ladies began to collect up their things, ready to go home, telling each other that their efforts had been very successful while they ushered the last of the lingerers out of the door. Volunteers would come in the morning and clear up and prepare the centre for the evening. Now everything could be safely left.

Serena, offered a lift by one of the helpers who lived outside the city, looked around her. It worried her house-proud notions to leave the place scattered with used mugs and crumbs and spilled soup, but since there were people coming to clear up...she started for the door with the last few ladies. They had almost reached it when Serena stopped.

Up against a wall in the shadows there was a bundle, but somehow it didn't look like an ordinary bundle. She went nearer to have a look and saw a child, little more than a toddler, dark-skinned, with black curly hair and very dirty. He was sound asleep.

All but one of the ladies had gone through the door; the one who had offered her a lift came to join her.

'We can't leave him here,' said Serena urgently. 'Surely his mother will miss him and come back? He's not Dutch, is he?'

'No, Bosnian, I should think; there were a lot of Bosnian women here, most of them with babies or toddlers. Shall I phone the police? I'll call in at Christina's and phone from there.'

She eyed Serena uncertainly. 'You wouldn't mind waiting here with him? I can't stop—the children…'

'Of course. As long as Christina knows where I am and will come pick me up later. I'm sure the mother will return soon.'

'Then I'll go. Will you lock the door?'

'No, otherwise if she comes she may think there is no one here.'

It was quiet once her companion had gone. Serena went and looked at the child, still sleeping. She looked round for a chair and found a wooden one in the room at the back of the building. She took it back and set it up against a wall facing the door, picked up the sleeping child and sat down. The chair was hard and the child was surprisingly heavy, but she told herself it wouldn't be for long.

The minutes ticked away half an hour, an hour, and there was no sign of the mother, and presently the little boy woke up. He began to cry at once, bellowing his fright in a language Serena couldn't understand. Certainly not Dutch; if he was Bosnian then this wasn't her lucky day. For want of a better idea she spoke to him in English, which didn't help matters, although he stopped crying for a time while she sang all the nursery rhymes she could remember. And there was not a crumb to eat or a drop of drink, other than the water which dripped from the solitary tap in the bare little kitchen. And when she tried to put him down so that she could fetch some he roared and screamed so much that she gave up the idea.

'The police will be here soon,' she assured him, and hoped that they wouldn't be long.

But the lady who had promised to go to Christina's and phone from there had found her away from home and, rather than explain to Corvinus, had driven on home. In the small flurry of finding one of her children had cut her knee, she had forgotten all about the matter, a fact of which Serena was unaware—and a good thing too!

Another hour passed. The child slept again and she turned over in her mind what was best to be done. There was little noise from the street outside; she had tried calling but no one had answered, and she hesitated to roam the streets, knocking on doors to be confronted by people who would probably not understand a word she said. They might even think that she had kidnapped the boy. It was a silly situation, she reflected, but surely the police would come, and if Christina had been told she would come too. She decided that she would wait for another hour and then try to find someone to help her. It would be difficult, for she would have the boy with her and he wasn't a passive child.

He awoke then, and burst into tears once again, wetted himself, and then was sick all over her skirt…

Mr van Doelen, home from Luxembourg, wandered into his drawing room and found it empty. He turned to look enquiringly at Wim, who had hurried after him.

'*Mevrouw* went this morning to help at that new centre for young people. I drove her there, and it's not in a decent part of the city either. I didn't like leaving her, but she said she'd get one of her friends there to drive her back. Teatime she said. But she ought to be home by now.'

'Probably having tea with someone, Wim.'

'Oh, no, *mijnheer*, she would never be away from home if she knew you were coming.'

'I'll phone around and see where she is.'

It wasn't until he had rung several of Serena's friends and been told that she had certainly been at the centre and as far as they knew had left when they did that he began to worry. And Christina wasn't home. She had been the first person that he had phoned; now he phoned again. She had just returned. 'Wait while I ask if anyone has left a message,' she told him.

She was back very quickly. 'Anna opened the door to Mevrouw Slotte—she was helping at the centre—she said she had a message for me but couldn't stop to tell Corvinus. I'm going to ring her now. I'll phone you back…'

Ivo curbed his fierce impatience. It was several minutes before Christina rang. 'The silly woman—says she forgot. Serena found a small child just as they were leaving—the others had gone on ahead. It was asleep and Serena said she would stop until the mother came for him. Mevrouw Slotte said she would call here and let me know, and also tell the police. She forgot all about it when she got home—some small domestic crisis, she said.'

'Thanks, Christina. I'll phone the police and go there immediately.'

'I'll phone the police; you go and fetch her. There are too many undesirables living around there…'

Ivo was out of his house, shouting to Wim as he went, and driving to Den Haag as though the devil were at his heels. But as he went through the door at the centre to all appearances he was his usual, calm, unhurried self.

He saw Serena at once, of course, sitting with the child, sleeping again, on her lap, and saw her face light up with joy and heard her voice, a bit squeaky with emotion. He crossed the floor, lifted her and the boy out of the chair and sat down, holding them both close.

For a moment he didn't say anything, but he kissed her instead.

'Oh, Ivo,' said Serena, and kissed him back. Then added, 'He's been sick all over my dress and he's…'

'Trifling matters, my darling. You're all right? You weren't afraid?'

'Not at first. I was just beginning to get scared, only you came. You called me darling; did you mean to?'

'Of course I meant to. I've been wanting to call you darling since the moment I set eyes on you—' He broke off as two police officers came in.

Ivo put Serena carefully back on the chair and picked up the boy, and she sat there, strangely content, smelling dreadful, listening to him explaining to the men. Presently he handed over the child to one of the officers and came with the other to where she was sitting. The officer understood English, and Ivo filled in gaps when Serena got stuck, and presently the police left.

'We are going home,' said Ivo. 'I'll lock the door and let Christian have the key.' He held out a hand. 'Come, my love.'

She looked down at her ruined dress. 'The car— I'm filthy…'

'Take it off.'

No sooner said than done. He cast the garment into a corner and took her hand without appearing to look at her, and he had her into his coat, out of the place and into the car before she could utter. Somehow it seemed quite a normal thing to be sitting there in a flimsy slip under his coat while he drove first to Christina, with the key, and then home.

Wim, opening the door, took one look and retired discreetly to the kitchen. 'They won't be wanting their dinner just yet,' he told Elly.

Serena made for the staircase, but Mr van Doelen was too quick for her. She was held tight in his arms, her face grubby, her hair a disaster, in a slip that would never be the same again.

'Did I ever tell you that you are beautiful?' asked Ivo, 'And that I love you to distraction?'

'No,' said Serena, 'you didn't, but you can tell me now. No, wait until I've had a bath and got into clean clothes.'

He sighed. 'I've waited so long I suppose that I can wait a few minutes longer.'

She leaned up to kiss him. 'I love you too, you know.' She studied his face. 'Shall we be happy ever after now?'

His kiss gave her the answer she wanted.

Modern Romance™
...seduction and
passion guaranteed

Tender Romance™
...love affairs that
last a lifetime

Sensual Romance™
...sassy, sexy and
seductive

Sizzling Romance™
...sultry days and
steamy nights

Medical Romance™
...medical drama on
the pulse

Historical Romance™
...rich, vivid and
passionate

29 new titles every month.

*With all kinds of Romance for
every kind of mood...*

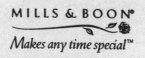

MILLS & BOON®
Makes any time special™

MAT3

MILLS & BOON

Tender Romance™

MASTER OF MARAMBA by Margaret Way

Needing a bolt-hole Catrina Russell jumps at the job of
governess on a North Queensland cattle station. She isn't
Royce McQuillan's first choice, but Catrina and his
daughter instantly form a special bond. His own feelings
are proving much more difficult to fathom...

MARRYING A DOCTOR
The Doctor's Girl by Betty Neels

Loveday West didn't expect to fall in love with Dr
Andrew Fforde but he was just so handsome and
charming. But is her place in his life temporary?

A Special Kind of Woman by Caroline Anderson

Single mum Cait Cooper has seen her daughter off to
medical school. Enter Dr Owen Douglas, who sets about
giving her more fun than she dreamed possible!

HIS PERSONAL AGENDA by Liz Fielding

Troubleshooter Matt Crosby has been hired to find
information to discredit Nyssa Blake – and stop her
campaign to save a valuable old cinema. But when Matt
meets Nyssa he falls head over heels – and his agenda
suddenly becomes a lot more personal!

MARRIAGE POTENTIAL by Emma Richmond

Kerith is certain she won't like Tris Jensen – his
reputation has preceded him. But she can't resist his little
son, Michael, who wants Kerith as his new mum! And in
no time, Kerith has Tris thinking about marriage again...

On sale 5th October 2001

*Available at most branches of WH Smith, Tesco,
Martins, Borders, Easons, Sainsbury, Woolworth
and most good paperback bookshops*

0901/02